THE LEOPARD

"An imaginative triumph."—*Time*

"Mr. Reid uses words as though
no one had ever used them
before and his prose is as fresh
as spring buds unfolding."
—*The Times* (London) *Literary Supplement*

THE LEOPARD

Victor Stafford Reid

with an introduction by
Gregory Rigsby

COLLIER BOOKS, NEW YORK, NEW YORK

The Macmillan Company
866 Third Avenue, New York, N.Y. 10022

Collier-Macmillan Canada Ltd.
Toronto, Ontario

The Leopard was originally published in 1958 by
Viking Press, Inc. and is reprinted by arrangement.

Library of Congress Catalog Number: 70–160085

First Collier Books Edition 1971

Printed in the United States of America

To Anne

Introduction

THE ENGLISH-SPEAKING West Indian novelist emerged in the 1950's. Mittelholzer, Lamming, Naipaul, Selvon, Hearne, Mais and Reid are some of the authors whose works enjoyed serious critical attention during this decade. Unfortunately, these names mean little to the average American reader despite the fact that West Indian blacks have always been involved in the history of the black man in America. Claude McKay and Eric Walrond (in a much more limited sense) are perhaps the only two West Indian novelists who have been widely read in America, and they lived in America. This is not to say, however, that Afro-Americans have been unaware of the West Indian presence. Indeed, American blacks have a definite image of the West Indian —a violent, outspoken, black-conscious revolutionary. Marcus Garvey is the prototype. In the literary world, as early as 1859, Martin Delany in "Blake" depicts a West Indian black as the organizer of a revolution to overthrow slavery. This idea of the militant West Indian is again portrayed by Du Bois in *The Dark Princess* (1928), and Ralph Ellison in *Invisible Man* (1952) crystallizes this image of the West Indian as a black nationalist in the person of Ras the Exhorter who later in the novel becomes Ras the Destroyer.

Victor Stafford Reid seems to confirm this myth of the West Indian revolutionary, because this Jamaican novelist, in true "West Indian revolutionary spirit," chooses rebellion and uprising as his major themes in his two published novels. In his first novel, *New Day* (1949), Reid focuses on the celebrated Morant Bay uprising in 1865—a rebellion by Jamaican blacks against that infamous colonial ruler, Governor Eyre. The second novel, *The Leopard* (1958), is set in Kenya during the Mau Mau rebellion (1952–1953), and though the central action of the novel concerns human conflict and change, the Mau Mau Revolution is ever-present in the mind of the reader.

The Leopard is a novel of chase in four stages. The novel begins with a band of Mau Mau Liberation Fighters hunting out the white man, who has usurped the indigenous African's land. The focus is then shifted to a particular Mau Mau revolutionary, Nebu, tracking down and killing a particular white man, Bwana Gibson; and then follows the third and major stage in the chase—the leopard stalking Nebu and his half-white son. Finally the chase ends with the white settlers pursuing the Mau Mau fighters and coming upon the dying Nebu in a cave.

Through the use of a rich poetic style, Reid invests this chase with an almost supernatural significance and transforms the chase into a quest—a journey of the black man in search of POWER. Nebu is the black man, primal, "struggling out of the bowels of the earth," seeking an unholy grail—the white man's gun. The power to destroy had made gods of the white men; at least, so Nebu at first thought. However, he is to discover that these beings were not gods but devils, for what else but evil could inculcate the powerless disgust, the hate that festered in Nebu's soul: "[the white man] was a *gun*: he hid a mile away behind a tree and slew you. And you were able to hate him as you could never hate a lion. For a lion never ignored your customs, or laughed at them." Nebu is to learn finally that power for the black man does not essentially come out of the barrel of a gun but from the inner disciplines of patience and the ability to accept change. The patience Reid speaks of is not the "we-shall-overcome-someday" passivity; rather, the cat quality of waiting in silence until the right time to kill. And the acceptance of change does not mean the losing of one's traditional culture, but "the strength to lose an age and gain a generation." Thus it is that the central image of the novel, the proverbial leopard whose spots cannot be changed, symbolizes cowardice and must die.

The plot is centered not in a story line, but in character movement and interaction. In terms of Nebu, the novel moves along the archetypal pattern of crime, guilt, suffering and revelation. Nebu's crime is a combination of sex and violence: he has committed adultery with his white mistress and has hunted down and murdered his white master. "Paying penance was important to Nebu. It was the law." And so a guilty conscience hounds Nebu until he decides to pay the debt by surrendering his own son to Bwana Gibson's tribe—all of Nairobi. The suffering that ensues on this purgatorial journey is both physical (a bullet wound that spreads poison to his legs—swollen and blue) and mental (a son who taunts, despises and humiliates him). And always there is the felt presence of the leopard waiting to pounce on Nebu when his wound weakens him to the point of defenselessness. After the pain and suffering, the hate and humiliation, comes the vision —pride. Nebu's journey could, with obvious modification, be the odyssey of every black man in America. The vision is not always the same but the journey is familiar—the black man's epic struggle to survive in a world hostile to blackness. "The white man has no understanding! cried the African angrily in his head," and the head that contains that thought is every black head in America.

Du Bois in his *Souls of Black Folk* said that lurking in the breast of every black man is the fear that he is indeed an inferior human being. That is the tragedy of Wright's Bigger Thomas and Baldwin's Rufus; it is the tragedy of Nebu. In an effort to preserve his humanity, Nebu keeps reassuring himself that in the bush the white man is nothing but a child, even as the black man feels himself a child in the white man's world. Moreover, he is stung to the core when the white man treats the black man stumbling over the English language as a laughing spectacle. On such occasions, Nebu would recall "the sweet poetry of his people singing at the spring ngoma," and he would turn to look at the young overseers, "the wish to torture bright in his eyes." This is a man insecure of his worth, and this insecurity becomes even more evident when Nebu loses the bwana's track. At once this bwana, whom Nebu was all along describing as the "pink fool," suddenly this "infant in the bush" became for Nebu "a son of god who had taken wings . . . wiser in the bush than even a Kikuyu." Indeed, under the influence of the truth serum of pain, Nebu admitted to himself that he was sorry that he was a nigger. And it was on this insecurity that the power of Koko (the leader of the Mau Mau Freedom Fighters) lay. In the presence of his men, Koko would scream to a captured white policeman, "Bow down to us, to Africa—you unlikeliness! Free my young men of the Strange Feeling—teach them how to stand while the bwanas kneel in the mud!" And then Koko would make this white man "beautiful" (death in Mau Mau fashion). It is this "strange feeling" which Du Bois identified in the souls of black folk; it is this "strange feeling" which Garvey sought to uproot from the hearts of black men when he dubbed them the "First Sons of the Earth"; and it is this same "strange feeling" which makes the black man today shout out so obvious a fact—"black is beautiful!"

In a sense, this is a novel about the black man's insecurity, an insecurity that is deeply rooted in his relationship with the white woman. Perhaps Reid is projecting onto the African a problem that is rightly that of the New World black man. But the problem of the white woman that is faced by Wright, Ellison, Baldwin and other Afro-American writers is raised by Reid in this novel.

Nebu had enjoyed his young black bride whom his tribe had chosen for him, but then as a farm hand for Bwana Gibson he slept with his master's white wife. His black wife was killed by the pox, his white mistress by the hands of her own husband when she brought forth a half-black son. But these women are not dead. For even as Nebu is dying, they linger in his consciousness. Was the white woman sweeter as a lover? No matter the answer. What Nebu is really asking in the lower regions of his soul is whether he is indeed the stereotyped black animal lusting after white flesh. Was he substantiating Thomas Jefferson's "orangoutang"? This is Bigger Thomas feeling guilty because he is sexually aroused by a white woman.

The spirit of the white woman pervades the entire novel. The white woman is the new Eve who will cause the fall of the black man as LeRoi Jones dramatically presented it in *The Dutchman*. In *The Leopard*, it is the white woman who really is the downfall of Nebu. It is because of his sexual relationship with her that Nebu feels guilty and cannot kill Gibson before Gibson gives him a gunshot wound which proves to be his undoing; it is because of the white woman that Gibson hunts down Nebu; and it is the white woman who bears the deformed child who is a thorn in Nebu's side. Moreover, Gibson made it appear that the Mau Maus had murdered his wife—the first Mau Mau killing—and this precipitated the whole bloody business of the Mau Mau Revolution. The white woman is the catalytic agent for a chain of misfortunes. If the black man is to start his new world, he must beware this new Eve.

For the Afro-American reader, however, the most compelling character must be the half-white son of Nebu. He is no tragic mulatto in the tradition of Langston Hughes and Nicolás Guillén; rather, he is the unnatural one who hates his blackness and cannot have his whiteness accepted. He is a "twisted little cripple" who tries to murder both his black father and his white stepfather. He cannot change, for like the leopard he is spotted—black and white.

The half bwana is the bastardized Negro in the Western World seeking integration but being rejected by the white man. Thus, when the half bwana tries to kill Bwana Gibson, it is not because he hates Gibson the white man (actually he wants to be accepted as a son); rather, it is an act of self-defense, for the black stepson knows that the white man's intention is to destroy him. On the other hand, the half bwana hates his father Nebu because he is black—"a filthy Kikuyu!" This is the self-hatred of the Negro, hatred for every drop of black blood. Witness how the bastardized Negro always describes himself as "half-white," never as "half-black." Symbolically he is a cripple unable to walk on his own legs: he is both the white man's and the black man's burden. However, he is not a man searching for his identity; he knows who he is. Speaking to Nebu he asserts, "You are my father." More than that, he admits to Nebu, "You love me very much." This is indeed the westernized Negro; he knows who he is; he knows that Africa is his fatherland and would

accept him as a black man. It is only that he wants
to hold on to his bwana culture, his bwana attitudes,
and so Nebu rightly accuses, "You are false! False!"
Only when the half bwana can accept his blackness
even as he acknowledges his whiteness is there hope
for his crippled soul.

This black-white tension is at the heart of the
novel. There is the white supremacist attitude of
Bwana Gibson who sees his houseboy as a "black
ape"; there is the black man-white woman relationship as the black boy consumes his white mistress in
a passionate abandon to animal sensuality; there is
the exploitation of black Africa by avaricious white
men who would rape the land for its gold and the
black woman for her passion; and there is the pa-
thetic mulatto, the half-white son of Nebu, who
hates and tries to murder both his black father and
white stepfather. This is a universe of racism which
breeds death and madness.

But the novel finally transcends race and roots
itself in the heart of man, exploring that nightmarish
and grotesque facet of the human soul. It is the
story of man confronting evil at its most dangerous
level, the evil that is part of his own human nature.
The relationship between Nebu and his son domi-
nates the book, and this is a relationship between
two human souls in a frank community of hate and
pain. This mutual hatred between father and son
represents that self-hatred, that self-destructive urge,
in man. Ironically, Nebu seeks out his own death
(for the gun he tracks down causes the fatal
wound), and the half bwana kills himself (for he
unloaded the gun that could have saved his life).
They were both driven to suicidal action even as

their cutting at each other was actually each cutting at his own flesh.

To help set the scene for this drama of murder and hate, throughout the novel Reid creates an imagery that is ghastly and sickening. There is rotting, pus-infected flesh that stinks, symbolic of the ugly, hate-deformed soul of the half-white boy, representing both the racist attitudes of the half-mad Gibson and the vengeful and angry spirit of Nebu; the landscape for the most part is hostile and ugly; the love act is pure animal passion in which a wife becomes a "white bitch" and a son "a twisted little cripple"; and the action is motivated by murder and slaughter—blacks massacring whites, a son always trying to murder his father, a husband slaying his wife, pox wiping out a village, a leopard stalking man and killing him. Within this heart of darkness, the hunter becomes the hunted and man surrenders —wounded and withdrawn in a dark cave. But it is not all horror and darkness, for out of this confrontation with evil there is an ambiguous illumination: "you could pocket a sunbeam easier than lure the march of change into a war pit." This theme of change is effectively demonstrated in the bow and the gun. Nebu finally learns to accept the fact that the age of the bow is gone. This is the age of the gun. So the dilemma arises: must the African, then, surrender his traditions (the bow) and adopt European civilization (the gun)? The gun was Nebu's undoing, and in spite of his assertions that change is of paramount importance in the ways of nature, his last prayer is for "long knives"!

For a long time, the words "Mau Mau" connoted savagery, brutality, sub-human torture—all characteristics of the African who had lost his one step into civilization and who had slipped back into his barbaric state (Robert Ruark's *Something of Value* is a typical treatment). *The Leopard* is an answer to this white racist propaganda, and a lyrical answer it is, free of the bombast born of bitterness. The blacks are heroic revolutionaries refusing to be dispossessed of their land; defending the right to believe in their gods (even if the white man believes that the African drums have deafened these gods); and rejecting the white man's god who has to be smoked out with incense and who needs lighted candles to be seen. The whites, on the other hand, are callous bullies, killing the defenseless, treating men like animals, boasting of their European civilization and yet living in Africa. They have transformed the African landscape into a land "rich in hate," proclaiming even God hates the black man. But Nebu refuses to accept a racist God: "We stand before him without skins. None is white or black."

Yet for all this loading of the cards in favor of the blacks, Reid succeeds in making the villains more than just unsalvageable white devils; they are part of the process of painful change—the industrialized twentieth century reaching out its destructive tentacles to all corners of the earth (even to insignificant Barbados in Lamming's *In the Castle of My Skin*, Collier Books African/American Library, 1970). Colonialism breeds injustice and inequality, but before one can attain full self-consciousness, one has to pay one's dues. *The Leopard* is a story about the paying of these dues. We know that the days of white domination of Kikuyu land are numbered, for the white men are "few as a handful of pebbles" and the blacks "number as the sands of Kilindini," yet, as the half bwana observed, "[the white man] is useful." He reviles and ridicules the black man; yet it is his bullet that stops the leopard about to spring on the dying Nebu.

There is hope after all. The white man might yet learn brotherly love (the ostrich flying by its own wings). Beyond the racial consciousness and national awareness, there is man searching for love which is the side of *The Leopard* that is left untold. Reid was not merely celebrating the heroism of his black ancestors, nor was he only protesting the social injustice suffered by the oppressed; he was pointing up the human emptiness when there is no love.

The only hint of love in the novel is the black man's love for the soil. Reid imagines an Africa (until 1962 he had never visited the African continent) whose valleys are vast enough to contain the world's sins, and whose earth speaks "dark secrets" to the naked soles of African feet as they go "down into the bowels of the earth," much like Césaire's Négritude "plunging into the red flesh of the soil." In the final analysis, however, *The Leopard* will be remembered as a novel in the Pan-African tradition, for here is an Afro-Caribbean writer writing within an African situation with an urgency that would appeal to the Afro-American scene today.

GREGORY RIGSBY

Howard University

PART ONE

Chapter 1

THIRTY WERE in the band that hit the Loman farm before daybreak. They slew all in the household and looted it of food, guns, and ammunition and vanished into the bush again, and nobody shouted *There they go!* because it was a sweet time for them to strike, when the morning ebb had drained the vigilance from the beleaguered settlers. But the looters found only three rifles.

Now three rifles were not enough to arm the gunless ones, so Nebu, who had joined General Koko's camp just four forays before, went without a rifle. And puzzled at his constant ill luck he now ran in the wake of his fellows as they entered the forest behind the farmhouse. Once among the trees, the troop took up the swinging trot that would put some twenty miles behind them by the time the morning patrol from Nairobi discovered the raid.

You would have noticed how the unshod black feet fell absolutely only upon those parts of the trail that were hard as stone after the long drought. And how the men ran with their elbows devotedly glued to their ribs so as to shed no green leaves from the trees for the sharp-eyed police trackers to see. They ran in a tunnel of safety. They ran into a stream in a splashing commotion that quieted as the long line snaked into the middle where the water rose to their armpits. Rifles held high above their heads, they breasted downstream for a mile to mystify the police dogs which would soon be nosing forth from the farm. They left the water by swinging up into the limbs of a squat, wide-spreading mango, going over from tree to tree as you cross the roofs in a city, and when they took to earth again they were half a mile away from the stream. A few colobus monkeys woke high in the trees and hugged their neighbors in beady-eyed teeth-exposed chatter concerning the ghostly line moving along the forest floor underneath, and subsided when they had passed, and that was all. Just a puff of lethal dust that had by pure chance carried over the Loman farm.

Chapter 2

Now NEBU thought and thought on his bad luck and found nothing to justify it. For in the troop he had played his part well, silencing a stubborn black servant with a thrust of his spear and providing cover for those whom Koko had chosen to perform the beautiful thing on the settler, his wife, and his whip-wielding overseer. But when afterward they searched the house, they found only three rifles and many bullets.

O, it took only a mile to want, but it took ten miles to obtain. A man could in his green time gather a hutful of needs in the crown of his head and force them crosswise and downward through his body until he grew heavy with it, but nothing would come until the time was ripe. Yet it was true that a man needed a rifle to fight the pink-cheek soldiers.

All of whom possessed all sorts of wonderful

weapons to stay out of sight and pick you off with ease.

If you got close enough up to them, then it could be the duty of your knife.

Some Kikuyus who had done this splendid thing spoke of how beautiful the white men became when they saw the *panga*, the long, sharp knife, purse its mouth to kiss their throats. But it was only at a great sacrifice that you could get up close.

At a sign from Koko, who was leading, they sank softly. Elephant grass grew thickly in that clearing up ahead, a fine place for an ambush. With eyes and noses and ears they peeled back every root of the clearing and rose only when they had proved it innocent of enemies: this was when, at Koko's signal, Nebu sent two swift arrows into the grass from his *wanderobo* bow. A flight of plovers lifted from the grass but it was the time for plovers to fly and so nobody had the gut-shrink. Yet they were wary when they rose, for the English had become good bushmen since the Emergency and were hitting them with their own tactics often.

In bone and flesh Nebu felt sound, but the rebuff to his spirit by the elusive rifle was real as an aching cavity. Each time they broke camp and headed south for their old Kikuyu land, it had seemed to him the Great One would relent and give to him what his shoulders and his fingers craved: the wood and iron of a rifle built to snuggle into your shoulder and to curl your fingers around and gently squeeze. But it was not to be.

Midmorning they halted by a stream and ate baked sweet potatoes large as footballs and drank the liquid that hissed and gurgled into their mouths.

They joked about the overseer whom they had tied to the gatepost while they looted the place and did all they did to his master right before his eyes so he would see what they would do to him. Koko, the leader, who called himself General Koko, said the overseer had been beautiful when they stopped at the gatepost as they were leaving.

On again they ran like dark blue wraiths through the tangled loops of lianas wrapping in rich laces gone shabby the straight-up trunks of cedars and tall *pruans*. They turned at the base of a magnificent copper-colored boulder and plunged up a slope of shale. And near where the land beyond the shale commenced to fatten up again for more forests, in a small cup of soil drift formed in a hollow of the shale, Nebu saw the imprint.

It was the imprint of a white man's boot, a thickly studded one such as the settlers wore on their farms. Nebu, running in the rear, dropped delicately to his haunches while the band ran on.

The imprint was well indented at the heel. The heel had sunk a good quarter of an inch into the cup. Nebu put his finger down but did not touch the print. The finger traced the outline in the air. Uncannily, he was singing, although no sound issued from his lips. The indrawn mask of his face tilted sharply up and he saw where the white man had stepped on harder ground after his single mistake. But farther up the Negro's eyes marked the passage of the man into the bush, by the improbable bend of a twig, the dank underside of a skidded pebble, loose earth a toecap had sent scudding to the hard-packed root of a silk-oak.

A white hunter perhaps, or a lost settler. He carried a pack, a heavy one, for see the imprint of the heel; and a pack meant many valuable articles. But the noblest of these would be a rifle.

It had all been willed by the Great One, who had seen Nebu's needs.

He stood upright again and looked all about him on land, and up at the wheelings of vultures and a tawny eagle crossing his patch of sky like the flick of a wrist. Sunlight in shafts plowed into the earth, pressing up into his nostrils the smells of the bitter purity of the womb where coal was smelted into diamonds. Nebu tightened the thong holding the panga about his waist. The great wanderobo bow was secure and comfortable at his back. The seven-foot spear at his side was snug as a good wife on a cold night. He buttoned the old pea jacket across his chest. The white man's trail bore upward. The Kikuyu began to follow it.

Chapter 3

FROM THE MOUNTAIN called Kenya (which has given the name to all the land) to the mountain called Ngong, and beyond it, is Kikuyu land. It is a land of immense folds and rolling parks; of water and forest and game; of hinged valleys so vast you could lose the world's sins in them.

The wind is hot and dry when it enters the continent at Mombasa; but it cools when it reaches the highlands, and they say it is like summer in Kent.

There are buffaloes and lions and rhinos and leopards and antelopes in the forests; great herds of eland and zebra, of wildebeest and giraffe roam the open parks.

In March, or sometimes in April, the long rains come, impregnating the earth with frightening fecundity, and the ancient wounds spread their lips again and new shoots spring from them.

It is a rich land: rich in humus and equally rich in hate, for all men crave it. Know, therefore, it is a land of feud: for the white challenger wants to conquer it, and the black man to keep it.

But none of the white men and few of the black understand it, or cope with it. Nor do any of the noble beasts, the lion or the rhino or the bull buffalo. Only the leopard understands it, for he avoids the strong and eats the wounded and the weak.

The trail was two or three days old, so Nebu knew that for now he could follow with speed and be unworried about caution. But his speed must be tuned to his strength, too; for when the time came for close stalking he must be fit and capable of closing with the quarry. He had all this carefully written inside his head, for it was the law.

In about six hours, the light in the forest would grow too dim for tracking. He could therefore run fast for these six hours, sleep very soundly and safely tonight in a high crotch of a tree, and run fast again all day tomorrow. The next day would be the time for stalking. He had it in his head as precisely as you or I would obtain a schedule from a railroad timetable.

At the outset it seemed easy, for the white man had not only walked in the wrong places, but frequently stumbled. The bush was no place for white men who stumbled. He had even walked straight across a clearing where it was unmistakable that a lioness and three cubs often lay about. Any *toto* old enough to walk would have smelled the place and carefully avoided it. Maybe it was a settler, but set-

tlers went for walks in Nairobi, or did their stum-
blings at a night-time *ngoma* with the beautiful and
conveniently unfertile Masai women.

Nebu knew the coffee-farming gentry very well.
He had been a retainer in one of the stone houses on
the Kenya slope, built where his fathers had once
herded their cattle. And as he raced forward, the
quiver slapping at his hip, his eyes relentlessly reel-
ing off each scuff of a boot, each rough brush of the
white man's leather trousers against the bark of a
tree, he was remembering.

He had come out of the bush after the Kaffir pox
had decimated his tribe, a muscled ebony youth of
seventeen, and had wandered into the motor road
and straight into the truck of Mulvaney, Bwana
Gibson's white overseer, who had been looking for
hands for the farm (five shillings a head for a
bonus).

"Young ones, Mulvaney, those we can break in
easily," Gibson had told him. "The older Kikes are
too set in their bush ways. You get no work out of
them after they have earned enough to buy themselves a snorter of palm wine. And—do you know
they resent us? Some of those oldsters wouldn't
mind cutting our throats. Do you know those niggers call *us* squatters?"

"Squatters!" Bwana Gibson choked on the fury of
recalling sweat and short-commons, the pains that
used to knot his bowels when the rains were late or
the nights so cold the coffee berries blighted, the
dreams he had at nights: he was a woman and the
bank in Nairobi that held his notes was a man bank,
pursuing him with that monstrous phallic pillar.

The bwana was in his prime then, strong and restless; and often he would be gone into the bush for days at a time, carrying only his rifle and a light pack. It was said by the buck-toothed Mulvaney, in the hearing of the hands, that the bwana knew the bush as well as a native and that not even a Kikuyu could out-track him. And the Kikuyus, whose pride and knowledge told them that this was a swelling of the truth, nodded gravely with Mulvaney.

Nebu dug irrigation ditches and wrestled mule plows until Bwana Gibson went home on furlough and returned with a wife. The old lick-and-promise ways of his bachelor days ended then. And Nebu, a strapping youth, was plucked from the field and planted in the house to scrub floors and move things. The woman had a firm seat on horseback and a great deal of fluency in her walk. She was a very young wife for the bwana, half his age.

Nebu the African turned away from the past and hearkened to what the present had to tell him. The sinews at his thighs roped and eased in smooth retraction at each stride. The Lawgiver within his breast pumped steadily along. He breathed calm as Sunday. He paid no attention to whether he was hungry.

The land had lifted very quickly and now the tall junipers and eucalypti were pointing proudly, kings of the highlands. Stringy mountain mushrooms appeared in the thinning undergrowth. Highland deer flashed about, too fast to shoot on the run. He hoped for an automatic rifle. He hoped the white man would have fitted it with telescopic sights. The black men called them the "woman guns" because of the way they talked fast and all the time and cruel as the Kikuyu women.

Nebu remembered the European policeman at the stockade in Kiambu whose joke was castrating captured Kikuyu. One night Koko went to Kiambu and took the policeman from his bed to the women deep in the Wakamba territory whose men had been eunuched. Deftly, the women kept the policeman alive for a week, but it became bad for the hunting. The game shied away from all that perimeter where the policeman's agony could be heard.

By those blackened stones at the foot of a clump of bamboos, it was clear that the pink-cheek had slept all night by his fire. Nebu's eyes raced beyond the stones and picked up the spoor again. The white fool traveled slowly, as if he had a week to breast the next ridge. A woman with child would have made better time. Gravely humming to himself, Nebu ran on, thinking if the rifle had a web attachment it would be more comfortable than the leather strap, which would hurt on a long march. Koko, who had two rifles, said so. Koko said he needed two, as leader.

The season of the long rains would begin any day now, he could sniff the wet in the afternoon wind, but he would catch up with his quarry before they came. The trail was fresh. It would be good sense, however, to draw in the reel as rapidly as he could, for sometimes the storms broke suddenly. The Msabu Gibson had not known how suddenly storms broke in Africa. For she had been in Africa less than a year, on the day.

Bwana Gibson had gone off on one of his trips

into the bush, and on that day his lady rode out for the field. Nebu the houseboy had swept and mopped the drawing room, of cut stone walls and mahogany floor, and had rubbed the tanned alligator skin pegged out above the fireplace. He jockeyed the squeegee into the dining room, the leaden foot stubborn and stiffly bumping along the narrow boards. He did the dining room and headed for the largest room in the house, the main bedroom.

It was hot working in the sodden pressures built up by the imminent rains; and Nebu succumbed to the heat and removed the red monkey jacket. From this to tossing aside the foolish red fez and finally the white shorts was the matter of a flip of the head and a fumble at the fly. The sweat prickled up hot and damp at every pore. He pushed open the heavy jalousies at the window and at that moment it seemed to Nebu as if the hot, sleepy earth breathed a gigantic, unceasing sigh. He stood stock still at the window as the freshening breeze pushed through the trees and laid the yard corn on its ears, rolled across the lawns, and flung the curtains stiffly into the room.

Vast, cold, furry hands instantly clamped themselves on every inch of his wet, naked body. He shivered violently at the first touch and then the bush flesh, which knew the elements with the primary acquaintance of a forest tree, accepted the wind with a gust of soft laughter. His head arrogantly cocked back on the column of ebony throat. Nebu laughed mirthfully. Miles away he heard the swiftly growing roar of the rain as it exploded on the sounding board of this wide and cushioned land.

Then the flood struck down on the trees outside and the house fell on his ears.

Nebu flung the squeegee away from him, opened his arms wide, and bellowed laughter into the darkly wet void which his land had become. And suddenly it was a ngoma, but a ngoma that not the wisest master dancer among the Somali or the Masai or the Kikuyu could conceive. For the thunder of the rains was the drums, the whistle of the wind was the pipes, and although he was the only dancer at this ngoma, he was all the tribes in all the land from the borders of Ethiopia and Uganda to beyond mighty Kilimanjaro.

He danced full of power and able to perform impossible feats of agility in time to the rhythm of the rain drums. The wind blowing on his nudity was the sweet-skinned girl whom the elders of the tribe had chosen for him at that half-forgotten Dance of Puberty when he had proved his maleness. Outside the windows the earth was in a joyous uproar beneath the rape of the long rains. The rain found all its hollows and embraced the hillocks. It soaked the trees to the roots.

Nebu danced nude, narrow-hipped, the strong calves and plow-widened shoulders like dark old wine catching what light there was about. In an odd way as he glided, a tiger grace to his flanks, he seemed to claim the room: running his hand over the bedsheets, touching with his finger tips the things of her on the dresser, the lacy small clothes thrown on a chair—and then his dream world lurched. Nebu hooked his head around and stared into the eyes of the woman.

She had ridden in through the rainstorm and her clothes were soaked and clung to her horsewoman's body so she was all long flat legs and shoulder hollows, and breasts proud as Babylon. The water-stiffened felt hat was in her hand. Brown hair flecked with water tumbled to her shoulders. The black, posed catlike on his sprung knees, was sculptured in hard, young manhood. With the tip of her tongue, the msabu touched the rainwater on her lips.

The incline sharpened the way hills do before they meet a plateau. Nebu dropped back into the hill man's style, the legs swiveled outward and cut forward in a half circle that added up to a huge stride without great muscular effort, storing his strength. Up on the plateau, he raced forward again. He took a guava from the knapsack and broke it, holding the halves in his cupped fingers to suck as he ran.

By tomorrow, he should be up with the white man. Clearly the white man was an infant in the bush. He used a compass to tell him the way back to his camp, yet even the stupidest sheep, no matter how widely he grazed, knew the direction back to the fold. A good way to punish the white man would be to take him deep into the bush and turn him loose, no compass, a bow and spear. He would surely die. Just as they took the black man into their towns and made him lose direction by rolling him in their gutters and he never could find his way into the bush again. But this one was his, he would make him beautiful by tomorrow. It was ordained.

The lives of the children of the Great One were as ordained as the *Nyeri*'s. The Nyeri rose in the mountain and rolled powerfully every mile, but its strength was a joke, for in the end it was nothing. For after it had flashed its teeth into boulders huge as twenty houses and wiped out whole villages—after all this anger, did it not end in the sea? As was ordained. So, men.

Women had the wisdom of the earth which provided food for thorns and for the beautiful pine, for lion and lamb, and never lost. The lion ate the lamb who ate the grass which had the lion in the end. And even where nightly she was wounded by men, she filled the wound with growth. This land, his Africa, was a woman: for look how soon after the rifts were scoured to sand by the rain, grasses grew in them.

And right now he remembered the rough thrusts of the msabu's hips when she fought for him to fill her, using the rich language of her body to talk away his fears. And the unfumble of her fingers opening the blouse to offer and offer. Planting, blooming, and bursting while the rain lashed in at the window. Meanwhile in Mombasa, in the narrow cobbled streets built by the early Arab conquerors, the Negro policemen began evacuating the children of the English soldiers from a flooded schoolroom.

Chapter 4

"**T**HE PINK ONE ahead is a fool as all the pink ones are fools," the black said to himself next morning as he ran arrogantly braced on his heels, the legs scissoring under the wedge-shaped torso. The blue-black skin gleamed with health, the mask face had no expression. He had shed the old pea jacket, tying the sleeves about his waist so it hung down his hips like a kilt.

Nebu had slept well. There had been a rabbit for supper, cooked between heated stones over a fire that had no smoke. Then he had curled in the crotch of a tree and had awakened at the first light and picked up the trail. Now the sun was curving into the first quarter, the sky immense and blue and the treetops glinting. Proudly he thought how he had taken the trail at the cold end yesterday and had run it into warmth. By tomorrow it should be hot under his feet. The white man was slow, the signs told him.

The land was a book you learned to read.

Men, beasts, fowls, moonrise, the shape of trees were all explained in the book.

And only when you had learned all about the lacerated paths by which the primitives had come could you widen them, or pave them, or put up filling stations in them.

"All the pink ones are fools," the black said to himself as he sped on his mission. "They come in and laugh at our god and say to us: *Beat no more drums to your god, already he is deaf.* Then they bring their own god whom they must smoke out with incense or light candles to see. They are as few as a handful of pebbles, yet they say to us who number as the sands at Kilindini: *Stay in your pocket of a Reserve except we need you to plant our coffee.* Yet such fools would walk as lords of our land.

"Great One, *give us long knives!*"

I should sing my prayers to the slug, Nebu thought in shame, looking down at the mocking land. *I should sing, "Great Slug, give thy son, Nebu, long eyes.*

For the land had deserted him, left him blind for the springy grasses, their tender curves deliciously untouched, to mock. The grasses said, "Only birds have flown by here since yesterday, Weak-eyed." And the unbroken cobs agreed that no lumbering bwana had ever made a passage through them. Swiftly the black stooped and his long-fingered hands asked the tiny stones whether they had been disturbed, but their heads were smooth and shiny with dew; not even a deer had specked their surfaces with dust from a hindleg's kick.

The Kikuyu knew his strange land; how the rogue elephant could travel like a fawn when his mad cunning ordered it, or the impatient lion lie quietly all day watching a slow grazing herd. But the bwana ahead could know nothing of this; he was a stranger to the forest. Then did the white man carry in his pockets one of their machines that flew? For the white man had left no signs.

Holding the panga upright in his hand, his back bent double, the black ran the first small circles of a tracker looking for a lost trail. He ran in an ever-widening periphery until he was cutting great curves on the slope. He ran with the anger a dim pain at the back of his neck. He could see through the earth's surface clear into its bowels. He would root up signs from the bowels of the earth and with them choke the bwana who had fooled him into believing he was an infant in the bush. He threw himself to the ground, sniffing like a great dog at the mold. He leaped up again and ran upland, found only the dung of small deer, and swept east for a mile, his trunk arched backward behind the high-kneed lope, then cut north again and quartered the ground in quick little rushes from one place likely to show signs to another. It was futile. The bwana was a son of god who had taken wings to the snows of Lord Kenya. All the pink ones were wise, wiser in the bush than even a Kikuyu—

The black halted and held his hand up before his face and said inside his hand, "Here is Nebu, Father Slug." For then he had it.

Then he straightened up and down in himself and

looked around until he saw the grove away on his right and the big thigh muscles vaulted up as he shot forward in a sprint for the trees. The bwana whom he hunted was no fool, but a man wise to the bush who would be smart in the open places, but perhaps be careless in the trees. The black entered the grove with caution. And in there the land was talking to Nebu again and it puzzled him greatly that the bwana who had beaten him over the head with shame, back there in the open, was an ox in the forest. He must be a funny bwana, part ox, part fox. The sweet arrogance filled the breadth of his shoulders again and the sac at the back of his neck throbbed and stiffened. He was a warrior, wise and swift and the owner of Kenya. Nebu began to hum.

He ran across a narrow neck of marshland on a mat of papyrus which had been flattened by his clumsy quarry. His eyes gleamed cruelly.

This one must be fat and panting beneath his burden of leather boots and cans of sardines. But he thought of the pack with affection, for in it would be a rifle. The rifle had made gods of the white men. He would be proud to slay this one and would carefully put the deed into song and sing to his grandchildren when he grew old. He would not have been proud to slay Bwana Gibson for he had wronged *that* one. He had never done it with the msabu again.

But she had fixed a fierce tenderness in him and he would have fought lions with his hands for the white woman. With hauteur Nebu reflected that the sun had the same tenderness for the tiniest flower in the bush and sometimes sent a finger through the thicket to touch it.

One morning, Bwana Gibson had entered the breakfast room and seen him place the bowl of double zinnias at her place, and something about his hands on the bowl must have disturbed the bwana, for he had pushed it aside and, laughing irritably, said, "You know, your Kikuyu boy fairly worships you, Edith. The way he hovers about you." And she had quietly replied, "I know."

Leaving Bwana Gibson nothing to do but go on with his breakfast and after a while mumble into his spoon, "You've got to be careful of them. There's some trouble brewing in Nairobi. Some terrorist gang springing up."

And then there had been nothing more about it, for everyone was concerned with the outbreak in Nairobi. Nothing more until the night of the storm when the cedars and the chestnuts and the olives had howled and wept and died of broken backs, and rivers had raged over what had been roads, and the bwana went mad.

Nebu dug in his heel and braced to a frozen halt. He stood quite still after the panga was gathered in his hand.

From the top of a boulder, a leopard had bounded into the clearing and stood sideways, straddling the trail, the head turned toward the black. The blade breathed in Nebu's hand, a living thing, and he was bent as a bow. Purringly exposing its fangs, the hunter fixed yellow eyes unwaveringly on Nebu. The demoniac head never left off pointing at Nebu while the heavy tail lashed slowly. Nebu had the chill feeling that the leopard was *learning* his image. Suddenly it leaped into the bush, wanton cruelty in every wicked line, and the path was clean. Nebu let go of the rocks he had been breathing in.

Unaccountably, the evil slew of the beast's head had reminded him of Bwana Gibson; the night the bwana had become an animal, shrieking and battering in the flower face of the msabu as she lay spent and weak after the birth while Nebu crouched in the storm outside and peered in at them through the window.

It was chilly in the afternoon high up on the slopes. The air smote Nebu running along an exposed ridge and he put on again the old pea jacket. The wool warmed his shoulders. Heath grass waved cobs around his feet and there were blackberries about. The long legs were pistons below the flat, functional abdomen. He had run all day, slaking his thirst at water holes, and now he was tingling with it. He could smell it near, smell it in tomorrow. Perhaps even by sunset he would be up with the white man, for the white man was slow as a cow.

Now it is a fact that Nebu was hurrying toward a murder, but it did not appear that way to him at all. To him he was stalking a dangerous man animal. An animal you could never get upwind of, for he had no upwind nor downwind. He was a *gun*: he hid a mile away behind a tree and slew you. And you were able to hate him as you could never hate a lion. For a lion never ignored your customs, or laughed at them. A lion was even willing to share his land with you, provided you took the day and allowed him abroad at night.

A stone, unseen under the moss, raked the sole of his right foot and while he ran he listened to what the injured foot had to say. His body was a tool he frequently used to the limit these days and a flaw could hamper him fatally. And not only was there the danger of stalking a gunman on a lame foot, but Nebu was looking to the time when he re-entered Koko's camp bearing the trophies of his dead foe. He should be upright then, like a young palm. General Koko was all for walking upright. Koko, who had lived in the white man's cities, said that the blacks there affected a walk of bowed heads and shoulders to indicate that they were yoke-worthy.

"Have nothing to do with the white man—except to make him beautiful!" Koko frequently raved. "And he is only beautiful when he dies of Mau Mau!"

Koko also said, "When they do not humiliate you, my brothers, they laugh at you. Are you giraffes or monkeys that they should laugh at you?"

Nebu had been (only once) to an Adult Education class at Kiambu and had seen some tribal elders stuttering over the words in the white man's book while a couple of young white overseers outside the hut grinned in at the window. And when Nebu remembered the wineskin of words which would pour from the mouths of those elders at a tribal council, words whose whispers were the winds combing the heads of the taller pines, or thunder at the commencement of the seasons, or the sweet poetry of his people singing at the spring ngoma, he had turned to look at the young overseers, the wish to torture bright in his eyes.

Who saw our land in the morning, from Kilindini to where the snow flies? Nebu the warrior sang in

his head and along his veins as he ran. *Great Spirit,
give us long knives.*

He brought down a deer during the evening's soft
rush of small game hurrying to cover before the big
cats came out. He fetched the carcass into the clearing through which the white man's trail ran, and
crouched by the bole of a dead acacia to make a fire
and skin it. And the curve of his back grew rigid as
he stared at what he saw down there.

For amid the welter of crushed leaves and broken
twigs that marked the blundering way of his quarry,
Nebu clearly saw the print of a boot—a woman's
boot. The boot had slid from the rib of a wet leaf
and touched lightly in the earth, but it rang a thun-
derclap in the head of the black.

Eyes, Nebu cried silently, *where have you been
since yesterday?*

*Nose, why have you caught none of the scents
which the women of the pink skins bathe their
bodies in?*

Angry and ashamed, Nebu silently rebuked the
members that had failed him.

Pluck yourselves out, Eyes.

Fall away, useless Nose.

He crouched above the imprint of the boot,
brooding.

And early next morning, before the dew had dried
on the pale-bellied *mogan* grass, the white man was
in his eyes.

Chapter 5

THE WHITE MAN was in his eyes there behind the thorn *boma* where the smoke rose. He had camped on the edge of a stream, a stream that stumbled over too many rocks, it needed a knock on the head to make it quiet. But the man was a baby, a pink baby who owned a gun. For who would camp by a noisy stream that would hide the approach of your enemy?

The Kikuyu had run early and had come up with the camp soon after daybreak. He had slipped in closer, preparing for a quick rush, when he remembered that the slowest of white men were salty with their guns. He was stumped for an instant until recollection of the white man's finickings when he was on safari with his woman brought grave laughter into his head. He would let the white man *come* to him. So he wriggled through the grass until he was downstream from the camp.

Now all he had to do was wait. And he had all

the fearsome patience of his land: of the cats waiting like portraits; of maimed trees waiting to flourish when the ax man had gone.

His cheek rested on the seven-foot spear extended on the ground. He had unsheathed the panga. All his muscles relaxed, deliciously quiet. Only his brain was alive in unrelated fragments.

Koko is asking anxiously these days, "Is there much killing in Dagoreti? Much death in N'drobo? In Chipalungu? Nairobi?"

How can a man keep sheep these landless days with the rains turning more and more into the mountains?

Do the yellow bamboos bloom better in spring or autumn? Huts should be built of bamboo and thatched with juniper and sleep would be deep and scented.

Such fragments.

The fog was slow fog in this morning without wind, but the sun was vigorous higher up and day stood on the top of the trees. As the sunlight strengthened, some of the fog tore away in great hinged sweeps. A man on safari should be out and doing.

But perhaps he is doing his hunting on the belly of his woman, Nebu thought. It had been so in the Ngong hills when Bwana Gibson had taken his bride on safari. The tent flaps had hung down into the high morning and when you wandered near you heard the buffalo lappings. And Nebu had averted his head when later the red-faced bwana emerged grumpy and exhausted, and from the *cerval*-cat eyes of the woman.

A shaft of smoke shot up behind the *boma* when the coffee pot was removed from the fire. Now the woman would be pouring for her lord and they would be sitting together, nursing the warm cup in their hands. The African lay full length, listening to the ancient hymns inside the earth. A cricket shrilled at the bottom of a stone and he heard the beat of a beetle's bony wings. A small thing wriggled through the grass and the stalks sawed impatiently to be upright again. He had the bull-thonged bow with an arrow in it beside him, but he hoped to use the knife. Arrows whistled and warned. The white man's guns never warned.

All the great hunters of his land gave warning, except the leopard and the white man. O, look, now. The forests saw the coming of the wind when the sky put on cloaks and unsheathed the lightning. The small boar knew the lion was loose when the shadows deepened under the trees. The earth knew surely in what month would come the teeth of the long rains. But the bwanas stole farms without a wink, farms a day's journey to cross. The bwana, like the leopard, was a lesser cat, he was king neither of forest nor of plain. He slew sneaking, he killed the wounded and the weak. The bwanas come from other lands, rich lands of which they boast. Why don't they return and leave us our land which they revile and ridicule?

All these things Nebu thought and there was too much gravity in his hate to be hate, but more, the tragedy of a truth, so simply constructed only saints should build it or live in it. Both sides were full of sinners.

Chapter 6

WHAT NEBU SAW told him that the Great One had dug the white man in his bowels and made him rise from beside his woman and go off to find a place of privacy downstream, grunting like an ill-humored pig at the insecure stones and the soft sands of the river bed, which twisted his ankles. Nebu, hidden in the grass, listened to his approach, singing the death song away inside him, his big body twitching, learning through an ear pressed to the ground what the earth told him in the squeak of grass, the crush of pebbles, the angry whine of dis-commoded insects; the time when he should rise and kill.

He read the story of the bwana's approach and sent it down into the springy thigh muscles and along the arm that held down the panga flat in the grass. *The fat pig is ready*, at last said the stones and the sawing grass.

The black reared to his feet and the hand holding

the knife flew back. But for a winking instant, the assault was stayed.

For the bwana whose mouth took that whistling inrush of air, whose torn eyes poured its whites down the disordered face, was Bwana Gibson.

Nebu turned into stone for a year. It took all that time for Bwana Gibson's rifle to come up, before he was quickened into flesh again and drove in the knife. He reeled away from the flash of the rifle and hit the earth with a hard bump.

Hear me, Great Spirit, he cried exultantly even as the white man's bullet smote him, *all the plains are ours, the Plains of Athi, at the foot of Lord Kenya, on which the white man built his cities.*

And the mountains are ours. And the rivers. And the forests. And the animals.

All ours.

Nebu held the holes in his side and struggled to his haunches. The blood trickled out of both mouths of the wound, for the bullet had gone clear through. He pinched the holes shut in his fist. With the other hand, he loosened earth to make a poultice. His face a mask of indifference, he removed his eyes from the wound and turned them on the bwana who was babbling from the ground.

Nebu, who knew lunacy, saw it in the clear, flawless eyes which were at odds with the tortured face. The bwana was foolishly wrestling with the panga. But it was buried too deeply in his chest. The face went placid, then it twisted, swam away, and returned with the muscles all broken up.

I have made him beautiful, Nebu thought triumphantly.

A man should go away with the poetry of ease on his tongue, the black thought. Like a sapling going down in the quiet good-bys of leaves whispering; going down on a boon of wind that took it gently to earth. Not like the bwana; not like an unwilling old tree, quarreling inside its rotten bole, writhing and shrieking all the way as it fell, destroying right and left the young ones of the forest.

The bwana's countenance turned sick in the midst of an insane laugh. A small area of pain exploded in Nebu's side as a tissue tore when he moved. The mask face showed nothing as he looked coldly at the dying man. He waited for the pain to go from his side, gathering strength in his belly and thighs and knowing surely that soon he would tower to his feet and watch the bwana die.

Gibson screwed his eyes shut and grimaced as the agony closed in. The black turned his own eyes inward and watched how the dark tide of pain would be lapping at the vitals of the bwana. The heat stored in his loins would be turning cold as the line of the tide edged nearer. Pain was very powerful. It was known to knead men into forms that would make a stone laugh. The bwana grunted and drew up his knees. The blood stained all his chest and appeared at his lips.

Nebu bent closer, and suddenly through the agony on the bwana's face spread a cloud of recognition and hatred.

"Nebu!" he shrieked, the blood spraying from his mouth. "So the black ape comes to me as I seek him. Did you know that the bitch bore you a nigger baby? Ten years ago. I have come into the bush since then many times looking for you. This time I brought your son so that he could watch you die. Then I would have slit his throat. Die, damn you, so that he may see it. Then he will starve or be killed by a cat. I have told him about you. I have made him hate you so much that he would rather die him-self than see you live." Again the insane laughter which broke off sharply as a wave of pain clenched his mouth tight.

The bwana had no grace, Ncbu thought. Bwana Gibson had turned ugly going away. The bitter waters had gathered at the root of his tongue and left no room for the sweet poetry of ease. It sad-dened one to hear it.

Soundlessly, his thoughts concealed behind the mask, Nebu sang the death song for Gibson. He died hard, worrying the blade like a dog with a bone, grunting and heaving as if he too would stand on his feet, like Nebu. The Kikuyu thought of dis-patching him with a blow to the head but decided against it. He would want to tell General Koko all about these moments of the bwana's being made beautiful. He drew an arrogant breath. There was no pain. Gibson sleepily drew back his eyelids and looked at Nebu.

"Look—look at me, black swine," he said softly. "Dy-ing like a white man. Do you—see—me—beg-ging?"

But neither would I, Nebu thought, gleaming black eyes in his pitiless face fixed like lights on the crumbling features. *Why cannot the white man un-derstand?*

The bwana was going now, for sure. He had ceased to struggle. The blood-wet ground was a door on which his knuckles kept tapping, tapping.

The white man has no understanding! cried the African angrily in his head, and swiftly stooped and wrenched out the blade.

It ended for Gibson in a rain of pain that made his ruined body jump for the knife. Slowly, while it sank back, Nebu reached for the rifle. He had it in his hand.

Dew was on the barrel and it was cold.

Carefully he removed the cartridge belt from the inert body and strapped it about his own waist. For the first time, he remembered the woman. He wheeled to slip for cover and then he saw the boy.

Chapter 7

Nebu bristled with weapons. In his left hand he carried the alien piece, the rifle. His right held the untidy sprout of the spear and panga and the wanderobo bow. He pushed his hands with all the weapons toward the boy and they looked at each other across them. The black, straight-boled as a good tree, bulked up, heels together. The boy stood crooked, one shoulder reaching higher.

There is no woman, the eyes of Nebu the Tracker said ashamedly. He looked the boy up and down and saw the crippled foot. The heel of the diminutive boot which touched the ground had made him think a white woman was in the safari. The eyes of Nebu the Tracker were ashamed.

My son has but one sound foot, the other is a twig. A yell of obscene laughter broke out inside him. He could hear it. It stopped.

The boy was thin and neat and *gray.* He had brown hair curling like smoke so you could not see the ends. He never moved his eyes after they had stopped on Nebu; never looked beyond Nebu to the patch reddening on the ground. The black let down his weaponfilled hands and stood as an equal before the boy.

"How do you do?" the boy asked politely.

"The—bwana—is—weary," Nebu observed, dredging up the long unused foreign words so that they trailed muddily in his throat. "He is—gone—into the long sleep."

The boy said, "You killed him, didn't you?"

Nebu bowed his head slightly in silence.

"I would have, but I could not have got out of the bush alone. Are you a Kikuyu?"

"Half," Nebu said gravely. "My mother was Masai."

"You lie," the boy said like a bwana. Nebu thought he could be the chief of police in Nairobi. "The Masai never marry outside of the tribe."

It made the black flinch but he was on penance, for he had wronged the bwana who lay in the grass behind him. He had taken the bwana's woman. He said, "I farm on my father's side and I am a hunter on my mother's side. I am half."

The boy said, "How do you stand comfortably, like that? Can you ride a bicycle?"

There is much for you to learn, half bwana. You may stand this way for a day when you are a herds-boy, with the sole of one foot clamped behind the knee of the other to hold you tall in guarding the grass against a leopard going on his belly into the herd.

"How do you go into the bush crippled in one foot? Do you fly lie a bird above the trees?" Nebu asked.

The boy laughed pleasantly. "My father carried me. My father was a fool. Mad as a March hare. He hated me. He would have killed me if you hadn't killed him first."

The morning was hardening as birds woke and flew out to their businesses. Nebu stepped past the boy, and, crouching and dodging from bush to bush, legged it swiftly toward the boma where the bwana had made camp. He dodged up the bank of the stream and came in around the end of the thorn fence. His nostrils dilated at the *white* smells. There was no woman.

There were two rubber groundsheets still spread on the ground, and a knapsack, a coffee pot beside the fire, two cork helmets, one for a man and the other for a boy, an ammunition belt, and nothing more.

The boy hopped in behind him and went to the

fire and sat down, favoring the lame foot in his
lap.

"Why did you kill my father?" he asked Nebu.
"Because he is mad?"

Nebu remained silent.

The eyes of the boy went blank and the high
shoulder twitched forward for him to lay a cheek on.
He grinned boyishly at Nebu when sight returned to
his eyes. The boy touched a pocket in the short
jacket he wore. His brown eyes were brown doors,
locking in big and little secrets.

Paying penance was important to Nebu. It was
the law. You could slay with easy conscience an
enemy in warfare. But when you killed someone
whom you had already wronged, for this you paid
penance, by a dozen goats, or a cow and bullkin, or
a favorite wife. But there was nothing he could pay
Bwana Gibson with. All Kikuyu land had been
broken and thrown away. And to whom could he
pay? The policemen in Nairobi? The queen in England? The bwana had nobody, not even a son.

"This—you make a safari?" Nebu asked. "You
hunt?"

"He said we would hunt niggers for the bounty,"
the boy said. "But he was quite mad. You ever
heard of a hunter *carrying* a hunter?"

When you grow older, Nebu stated clearly and
silently, *you will wear false teeth and no shoes. You
are half a white man.*

"I am Nebu," Nebu said. "What do they call
you?"

The gray face paled. "Nebu, you are Nebu?"

And suddenly the boy shrank away and the high
shoulder came up. He buried his face in the high

shoulder and peered out at Nebu from under his arm.

He was hearing the music more frequently nowadays and it was no longer the dim strings at the bottom of the crocodile pool, muffled and wet, but the high, thin clarity which the little goat men plucked on their instruments way up on top of the mountains of the moon. Gibson, that flipping fool, thought he had been artful, but the black had got to smart bwana Gibson first. Could it be that this *filthy* Kikuyu was really his father?

The black was looking back at him. He ducked his head and peered craftily out again. That sharp nigger would pin him if he didn't watch out. *Careful,* wrote a hand on the brown doors of the boy's eyes, and they swung shut again.

"Did my fa-father speak back there?"

"No," Nebu said the untruth quietly. "The bwana was tired."

The eyes regarded him slyly from their half-concealed place. Then the boy straightened and looked fully at the Negro.

"I am the young bwana," he said. "Have a cup of tea."

"Coffee," Nebu said gravely, glancing at the coffee pot.

We, the people of the Kikuyu, cleared the ground and plowed it and plotted the cuttings that grew into this, Nebu sang in the deep as he placed the coffee pot on the coals.

"You have come from Nairobi?"

"All the way from Nairobi," the boy answered soberly, inspecting the clean leather sole that bottomed the shoe on the crippled foot. He looked up. "I say, you do ask a lot of questions for a black."

Nebu looked steadily at him until the brown eyes were taken off.

Whom do you pay to when there is nobody to collect? Nebu asked himself. *And what do you pay with when all your goats have been scattered? When there is nobody to collect, you pay to the tribe. That is the law from the Rift Valley to where the sun sets beyond the shoulder of Lord Kenya. In goats, or cattle or women.*

You paid in flesh, the law said, but Nebu had no flesh except his own bullet-torn body.

"Have your coffee, General Nebu," the boy suggested.

Nebu dropped down and poured hot coffee into the white man's cup and drank noisily, thirstily, the mug of hot liquid that scalded his throat with all that goodness, aromatic, strengthening, filling his empty belly.

The boy looked up and cried explosively, *"No!"*

Slashing his hand forward, he knocked the mug from the African's hand. Then the good foot kicked toward him with easy custom the discarded tin that had contained the condensed milk. "Keep that for your use."

Nebu hoped desperately that the hate pulling him to his feet would go away; but it swept him up. He was blind and lonely with hate and he groped for the young stranger who had put out his eyes.

"No!" the boy shouted so loudly it cracked his voice across. "No—Nebu, *no!*"

The cry went in and Nebu halted his hands inches from the boy's jugular. He stared at the scared flut-

ter of the pulse beneath the gray skin and the sweat
in the hollow at the base of the boy's neck, where
a blow from the edge of his hand would have divided it like a doll. The black slipped slowly back to
his haunches, his shoulders narrowed.

"Li-like the pox—you could catch the bwana's
madness from his cup just as you could catch the
pox," said the boy. He was still shaky, and the
strokes of his tongue lining his way out of trouble
were unsteady.

"I will use the bwana's cup," Nebu said softly.

The brown doors in the boy's eyes closed without
a click. "Of course."

The Negro rose and stalked upriver and went to
the edge of the water. The wound in his side spoke
to him. He breathed in deeply and it became quiet.
He swallowed on a sort of shame at the weakness in
a man that made him fool himself into believing that
the false fire was true fire, that wine power was true
power, that goats' ordure, being black, was diamonds.

The half bwana had not fooled him. He had
glimpsed the brown doors closing and he knew that
the boy was in accord about the bwana's cup only
because he was the weaker. But was a man's door
not meant to be closed? All men made their own
stockades of habits and customs, and they never
welcomed intruders. In the old, strapping days, who
among the Somali had ever drunk from the Kikuyu's
ceremonial bowl of calabash set on the shelf made
from the olive? The strapping days when the *morani*
had walked on their heels and boasted of the number of hostile warriors they had made beautiful.

The boy watched Nebu's back disappearing at the edge of the stream, then hobbled to the rifle which had been carefully stood against the trunk of a tree. Working swiftly, he removed something and put it into his pocket, his face contorted with hatred and anger. Then he went back to his place near the fire and lay quietly waiting.

The stream rushed and fought small splashing battles over the rocks, and ran hurriedly past the calms to fight farther downstream. Nebu returned to the camp to retrieve his bow and hunt a fat little one for his food. Then he remembered that he now owned a rifle. He grew and grew into a giant, seven leagues tall.

Chapter 8

THE RIFLE WAS everything it had promised in his dreams to be. The stock was sweat-polished, the heel grooved for shoulders, a front sight seeing through which you cut the sky into neat segments; for an instant you held an eagle in the steel-framed

windows; for a longer while you looked at a nob of
cloud that could be parted from the sky by a
squeeze of your finger. A godlike feeling. The thing
balanced in your hand faultlessly, built for you from
the commencement of time. It was such that you
wanted to sing.

Nebu dropped the gun into his lap and wiped his
forehead with the back of his hand. He could go to
bed with such a gun. He lifted it again and sank his
cheek to the cold metal of the barrel as he had seen
Koko do, and looked along the pure line to the end
through which the bullets went. There was the top of
a tree he could blow off, the head of a mountain he
could shoot away, a wood pigeon he could halt and
shatter. He was gifted with destruction.

He looked down at the gray-skinned boy. He
looked at him from the sound foot, up past the twig
of the other, uselessly thrown across the sound thigh,
over the interlaced fingers to the petulant, heavy-
lipped mouth and the brown eyes blank as tomorrow. *You, too, half bwana,* Nebu thought, *could be
broken quickly by the rifle.*

Nebu got to his feet and moved out of the camp.
"A fat little one," his hunger said, but the grand
dreams had awakened, bellowing in him that now he
was lord of life and death. He almost ran for the
bush.

Chapter 9

AND THE BUSH was waiting and drew him in with a hundred thousand green arms in heat for him. He looked back over his shoulder when the branches of a wild banana clashed behind him and then he swam into the green cave. He held the rifle familiarly, so often had he held it in his dreams. Now he had it in his hand and it felt familiar. He walked exalted, he was of the salt of the earth.

But his head said, *Seek signs, Nebu,* and the part of him that was hunter broke free of the false thinking and began to note the fall of the land and the way the brush opened for the animal trail to the water hole. The path had been pressed down by the great furry paws and the stomping ones of all the beasts who had gone down it to the drinking place, immemorially. The black slipped swiftly along, his fingers working tightly on the hard virginity of the stock, the stock that sank here and there into the simple dimples of the Masai girl, and he thought how soon it would tongue out the boom of flame and be a big delicious woman declaring for him.

It was yet early for the morning drink and occasional lave of the small fat ones, the bush pig and the deer, the spurfowl and guineafowl, the antelope and the gazelle, whose legs would snap like sparrows' but whose meat was fit for the kitchens of the Great Spirit. So Nebu made for a slight knoll one dozen feet from the edge of the water hole and with quick slashes of the rifle butt cleared out a nest behind a screen of shrubbery and folded himself into it.

Generations of wild animals had with hoofs and paws punished the earthen bank of the water hole so that it was giantly chipped and scarred like pottery knocked about. A frog jumped in the soupy water and launched forward, square-shouldered and high in front of the gray furrows it drew on the surface.

Behind his cover, Nebu was a dark legend waiting to come true. Excitement prickled sweatily from his pores and he wiped the palms of his hands on the pea jacket. He found firm places for his elbows and now he was a dark river of stone anchored into the earth and he waited in impregnable unyielding patience. He looked along the barrel again where the brave bullets would soon burst in a brilliant shower. He had learned many things from the bwanas. He had learned how with a small metal animal you could open a stolen can of peaches without disfiguring it on a rock. How, with a key no larger than the hiding places in the middle of his hand, he could unlock the stoutest iron door. How a pair of scissors could cut through tin as a knife cuts through a slab of butter. All knowledge that was wonderful and overflowing in splendor. Most Kikuyus in the bush had never even heard of such things. And the most wondrous of all was the metal animal he now held in his hand. The animal which the white man had mated out of his arithmetic and gunpowder and used to plow under his enemies. Just as the Kikuyu plowmen had done when they mated the buffalo and the bull and brought the strong and amenable half buffalo. Now he had it and he would learn to use it. *Firm places for your elbows.* Koko, who had two rifles, had been emphatic about this.

The first to enter Nebu's sights was a spurfowl and her brood, scampering fearfully to one of the tributary pools which drained through a fold in the bank. He framed the sight on the old hen, and his indrawn, fatal eyes in the excited mosaics of his face were candles shooting up and down in a windy room. And then, inch by inch, he lowered the weapon and the arrogant head came up from the barrel.

The black lay coiled immobile in his nest while his mind became a half-lit battle field in which ideas fought softly and died. A bush pig and an antelope and other food leaped from the forest to the table around the water hole and the sun thickened through the leaves, warm and yellow, flowing down the trunks. And he had this final thought: *It is unworthy of a moran.*

It was unworthy of a warrior that his unbloodied weapon should first be used on the fat little ones. Such a weapon was made for the royal lion, or the strong buffalo, or the sly, treacherous leopard who is schooled in ways of evading the powerful and going after the weak. So he rose to his feet and turned away from the water hole and went into the bush. And he looked for spoor until midmorning but found none that was fresh enough to draw him along, for he would not hunt far from camp. None until he had crossed the Valley of Smoking Skies, as he named it in his head because the dun clouds hung low, swinging between the hills like thick smoke.

It had a gorgeous floor of periwinkles and copper-red cineraria, and the loveliest tree in the wood grew there, the poetic *podo*, going up straight as a sun-beam for seventy feet and roofed in foliage as green as Eden. And on a low branch of the wild fig, whose tiny leaves shone like jewels, three spear lengths ahead of him, Nebu saw the ugly evil waiting for him, disfiguring the beautiful valley. Horrifying to him as a mamba coiled in a Communion Cup. Trained to be still at the unexplained flutter of a leaf, the Negro was fixed.

His eyes took in the leopard on the branch, the narrow forehead that bore a curious resemblance to the serpent's, the puff-stitched mouth like a badly mended purse, the front paws neatly crossed before the face. But the brute was perfectly at ease, no cobra swell at the neck, no quiverings at the shoulder, and Nebu commenced to bring up the rifle, had it at his shoulder and bearing on the leopard. Then, his breathing securely locked away for the present, he began gently to squeeze the trigger as he had seen Koko do. But he squeezed forever and ever and nothing happened, nothing exploded. The leopard lived, neat, inviolate.

Nebu pulled again, a little quicker this time, and

again, and again, but the white man's weapon would not speak for him. He jerked and tugged at the trigger, sweat piling on his forehead. He held it away and pulled. He looked down into the barrel and at the same time, at the risk of blowing off his head, jerked the trigger again. And in the silence his heart leaped six houses. His bowels went mad and knotted themselves into a pain he never knew existed. The hills closed in and crushed him, broke the bones in his chest, broke all his bones, and when the dust of himself had blown away and the sun gave light, he saw that the leopard had gone. The fig tree and the valley were both empty, and he was heartsick and washed in sweat and doubt.

For it seemed that Ngai, the All-Seeing, had forsaken him. Ngai, the All-Seeing of the Kikuyu, who lived on the highest places of the land, on Kenya and Juja and Aberdare and Ngong, but was present in all the children of the Kikuyu, had departed from him. Five forays had been made on the white intruders and he had failed to find a rifle, and when he had, finally, run a cold trail into blue heat, the rifle he had found would not speak for him. But he knew why he had failed. Crushed as he was into little pieces in the Valley of Smoking Skies, he knew why he had failed. Ngai had taught that the man who did wrong would not go unpunished, except he paid in the material he most loved, flesh of his cattle or his woman. And it was two times he had wronged the Bwana Gibson and not once had he paid.

And then, like trade winds rising, like the first crocus to blow, like the tawny pride of old wine that takes it slowly until the sudden onslaught in the blood, knowledge of how he *could* pay the debt was understood in Nebu. He had flesh, the coin of blood payment, and he knew where he would find Bwana Gibson's tribe to whom the payment should be made. The bwanas were all of Nairobi, or Mombasa, or Fort Smith at Dagoreti where the older Kikuyus had put up their fortified villages and slain the first inrush of the English who had come with Milord Lugard. He would regain credit with the Great One.

Nebu commenced his return to the camp and the hole in his side awoke and shrieked all the way. When he stumbled into the boma the boy looked curiously at him.

Chapter 10

THE LONG RAINS arrived in the early afternoon. Nebu had been burying the bwana, putting him under that the curse would go from the rifle. He dug the grave with his panga and gave up a couple of arrows to lie at the bwana's side, old things which he had been taught had virtue. He cast in the loose

earth from the feet upward and finally threw dirt on
the face. Then he wiped his hands free of dirt and
knowledge of the bwana. The curse should go with
that gesture. He heaved upright on his straight thin-
muscled legs and the pain at his side was balled in a
fist. He gasped and stood where he was until it flattened out. He turned his head away from the long
rectangle at his feet and listened. He heard it. He
heard the coming of the rain across the land, a clat-
ter punctuated by heavy reports of thunder. He
loped from there, making for the camp. The boy
looked at his hands when he came in behind the
boma, the first rains thumping down in lumps on his
uncovered head.

"You have brought no game," the boy said, his
eyes on the black's hands. "You are no good with a
gun."

Nebu dropped down and looked in at the open
brown doors before they were quickly closed. He
thought that in there he had seen a kind of laughter
folded back like a weapon. But one did not show
anger to a toto. The lion did not roar at a mouse.

"The Masai hunter has failed. Will the Kikuyu
farmer now dig roots for our meal?"

Not even when the little mouse gnawed at him
should the lion roar. The gray boy huddled farther
into the shelter of the lean-to they had built above
the groundsheets. The mushroom drops had changed
into the tremendous tears that would splash from the
sky until the sun shone again. Nebu reached slowly
for one of the sheets, his eyes on the boy. He saw the
dim flare of his nostrils when he closed his fingers on
the sheet and suddenly spilled it in the air, ridding it
of water and fallen leaves. He drew it down in a cape

over his head and shoulders and tied the laces across his middle. Snug as an egg, he gestured his thumb at the other sheet and rose. Slung on his back by the web attachment, the rifle poked up the sheet, cone-shaped. His wide-apart feet had been washed clean by the rain and showed the high-ridged bone shapes and the turn of the great toes that had crossed continents in bondage time and again. He looked a tall strange splinter from the past.

Nebu moved about, gathering items for the knap-sack. The boy asked in a high clear voice, "Where are you going?"

The Negro straightened. He looked down at him. He looked at the twig in the tightly laced boot lying out limp and he remembered how the bwana's trail had been halting. The white man had picked on a strange vengeance. If he had meant to hunt out and kill Nebu, he should have gone unencumbered into the bush. But perhaps the bwana had been jiggling in the head all the while, not only today when he had been made beautiful. The night of the storm when he had strangled the msabu he had plainly been mad. If the animals had not finally got to him, burdened as he had been he would have perished from fatigue. But no. No. Nebu remembered now. The bwana would not have perished because of the boy. Whether he had found Nebu or not, he would have disencumbered himself rather than run the risk of succumbing to fatigue and be easy prey to the clawed ones. Whatever had happened, the toto would have lost. Working it out in his savage un-sparing logic, Nebu came to that conclusion. The boy had been doomed from the beginning.

General Koko, who had lived in the white man's

cities, had explained to them that the doctrine of brotherly love which the white man preached from his god was like the wings of the ostrich. No ostrich had ever flown by its wings.

"Hear me, brothers," Koko said one day under the mimosa tree. "Hear me. The white man builds houses of death in every one of his cities. In some, there is a house for hangings, in others for beheading with a machine or an ax. In some they put their brothers into a chair to sit and then they send the electrical current through the chair and burn them to death. If they do that to their own white brothers, what will they not do to us?"

The boy laughed. Peculiarly.

Nebu peered through the rain. "Did you—laugh?"

"*You* will have to carry me, you know," the boy said pleasantly.

Nebu shook his head slowly, thinking out the laughter.

"When he groaned and stumbled under me on the bad trails, my father called me a legacy which he would soon be happy to lose. My father was not very fond of me. Sometimes I think he was afraid of me. In Nairobi, when I laughed and told him that the other children called me the Gray Rat, he put his fingers over his eyes and peered through them at me. They said he was mad because the natives killed my mother the night I was born but he managed to save me. Why do you think he saved me first?"

The rain had got inside his head and Nebu heard it roaring between his ears. The thick gray face looked out at him from the tented covering of the sheet, a smile curving the soft lips; the brown doors were swinging wildly. Nebu caught glimpses but he was not functioning.

"I was only an infant. I would not have *felt* anything. Why do you suppose he saved me?"

But the boy watched the Kikuyu stalk into the forest. And when he returned, his head bowed and face turned aside to avoid the long silver whips of rain elongating out of the sky, he bore a pair of stout staffs cut with a crook at the ends. He held them up before the boy and walked them forward in pantomime and then let them fall to the ground in front of him. Then he picked up the plastic folding cup which the boy had knocked from his hands, folded it down, and put it into a pocket of the pea jacket. He shouldered the knapsack.

His gray face rigid, the boy took a long look at the crutches. He rose with the aid of the lean-to, the toe of the crippled foot trailing, and he tried the crutches and found they were no worse than those he had used in Nairobi or during the early part of the safari before he had dropped them in the river where the crocodiles showed their snouts, with glancing hope that his father would go in after them. He smiled at the black and followed him out of the camp.

Chapter 11

IN THE TOWN OF Kiambu, in the concrete police post outside the cage of steel wire which was alive with black prisoners, the inspector of police agreed with the views of the Army lieutenant who had just come in convoy from Nairobi. He agreed that such a campaign could fold this band of Kikes in a fist. The hard-mouthed young lieutenant swiveled the chair and leaned back, now that his views were home.

"All we need is a competent guide into that part of the country," he said and looked the question.

"Gibson would be the man for it," the inspector said.

"Then let's get him."

"But Gibson has disappeared."

"Disappeared? Who is he?"

"A planter. Funny business. Happened a fortnight ago. He and a crippled boy—son—of his."

"You mean the blacks got him? Hasn't been reported, has it?"

The police officer shook his head no. "No. That is, we don't *know* it was Kikes. He just—vanished, he and the queer boy."

"Then it's the Kikes all right. Queer? What do you mean queer. Crippled?"

"Crippled? Yes, somewhat. A misshapen foot, I believe. But more than that—queer. Probably a half-breed bastard. But it's a long story. Before my time, actually. His wife was killed at the time of the boy's birth—whether by her husband or Mau Maus, I don't know. Could have been the first Mau Mau killing in these parts. House was burned down, too. The whole thing seems to have put Gibson off his rocker. We've never really sorted it out. But ever since then he's made frequent trips into the bush. Knows it like a native. The last time or two he seems to have taken the boy with him. Never would talk about his trips. There was a black mixed up in it some way—a houseboy of Gibson's. He disappeared about the time the baby was born."

"Hmm. Anyway, that won't help the price of fish. This guide now. The niggers will not be expecting us now that their 'long rains' have begun. We could knock them down with twenty-thirty men and a couple of mortars *if* we can move swiftly *and* surely through the infernal bush. Specially the bunch led by—what d'you call him?"

"Koko," the policeman said. "General Koko. I suppose we will be able to round up a good guide for you. Trouble is, now that they think the Emergency is over they all want to do nothing else but plant coffee."

The Army man rose. "Coffee? Remind them of the Lomans." Tall and wide, he was brutal as a castle.

Chapter 12

THE RAIN CLAWED and kicked, shrieked and roared on the roof of the forest. It lashed at the treetops and came sullenly down the trunks with angry fluxions of its glistening coat. Branches broke beneath its weight and it scoured out gullies among the roots. The storm had eaten the daylight, and in the dark, the watersoaked trees gleamed like knuckles.

Nebu sloshed along in front, massive and shining in the rain-slick rubber. The boy hobbled behind him. The boy walked with his head down because the crutches sank in the soft spots and it tired him to fight them out of the mud. The crooked foot was a loose piece dangling a bit behind him. But his eyes were bright under the film of rain as they lifted at intervals to the heels of the man in front. The boy did not want to lose Nebu.

Nebu spoke to the beetle in his side. The beetle itched around under his skin, scratchy as a leopard on a tin roof. The bwana's bullet had been powerful. Even if it had not stayed in you, because your magic had been too strong for it, it was powerful enough to leave a beetle under your skin to remind you that it had called. The rifle at his back made him uneasy. He had slung it on out of pretension. He had not wanted the half bwana to know how scared of it he was. But, cold and dead as it was on his back, there was no telling what mischief it could be up to. It possessed some powerful magic.

A thought like a piece of wire slipped inside the boy's head. Back there in the camp, the nigger had bent down to look into his eyes and he did not all the while trust his eyes. One time, on the in-trail, Gibson had surprised the look in his eyes and had never after that left him alone with the gun. Look, now. Notice this morning when he had gone downstream to find a crap-house, he had taken the gun with him? But a fat lot of good it had done him. The thought slipped inside his head that, just as the black had tried to read his eyes, he would read Nebu's mind through the soles of his feet.

Look at his big heels, like blobs of dirty suet pudding lifting and falling in the mud. I wonder what the nigger knows? The sole of his foot goes down into the bowels of the earth and comes up streaked with the dark secrets he carries in his nigger head. But the rain washes it clean before I can read it. The sole of his foot has eyes too. See how it evades the little islands of leaves and sticks? It knows that adders may lurk among the leaves.

He knew thorns which, if a man stepped on them, would send the poison leaping upward. Upward, until it closed about his heart. But he had no such hope. The black knew each inch of the land as a lion cub knew the tits. His—father—had worn boots up to his knees. He was right to still think of Gibson as his father. He *was* his father. The mad old fool had been lying when he had said that this—this—

He drew a big breath down into his narrow chest and felt big. Sometimes he wondered if it was wrong to be so big. Other people were content to be small and silly. Perhaps it was nicer to be small and silly. It was not always fun to know that, with one sweep of your best thoughts to the front of your head, you could kill one of the small sillies. He had fought more than once against the idea of killing Gib—his father—and had succeeded in returning it to its place in the back of his head.

There were also moments of weakness, when he was overcome with terror that the day would come when he would not be able to push it to the back of his head; then he would be alone in the bush. But at that time the little goat men on the moon would hold their sides and shriek laughter at him, winking that there would be room for him up there; he would not be left alone in any old bush. But he would have to bloody well fight hard to keep his best thoughts from the front of his head every time he looked at the black.

The rain whanged with enthusiasm into the open places, glad to meet the earth without having to fight a way past the trees. The torrents here descended uncontested on Nebu's head and rolled off the smooth mask face down his chest and gathered at his belt, soaking down cold on his genitals. He pushed out his lower lip and gulped in mouthfuls of the sweet water. It was water with gifts of pure upper air, flowing straight from the hands of the Great Spirit. It had abundant life, giving the tints to the lovely podo and making the lilies sing. The sun-bleached red soil had turned dark and, in some places, black. Later it would be fruitful, blooming in grass to feed the gazelles who would please the lions.

It had taken him not quite two days to get up to the bwana; but then he had been going flat out, running hard and full of spring at his knees and ankles, sound in wind, no hole at his side to be careful about. And at that time he had been big with certainty that an enemy had entered his country and been delivered into his hands. Now doubts wriggled in his mind. For the bwana had not been a true enemy. Bwana Gibson had really been the wronged one. Nebu marched old and hurt, looking for a cave.

Night, the true night, not the night of the rain and the trees, licked tongues into all the corners, and licked darkest at the mouth of the cave which Nebu had chosen for their shelter. It was bone dry, from just within the door. It went far into the cliff face. The black stood well back and loosed three arrows into it and heard them *spang* at the back. No animal came hurtling out. He gathered sticks inside the doorway and took the white man's gasoline lighter from the pack and struck a fire. No snakes. So he went in and recovered his arrows; the head had broken off of one. He built up the fire and took off the wet rubber. The boy had already sunk down, the crutches propped against the wall. Nebu motioned at the pack, and the boy, after a speculative look, worked at the straps. He did not look back at the African again.

The fire burned a great eye at the mouth of the cave. The black went out into the night and returned with pieces of deadwood which he stacked for the all-night fire. He caught rainwater into the pot and stood it on three stones at a corner of the fire. Coffee was in a large brown tin, a slab of bacon wrapped in grease paper. There were tins of flour and sugar and several of corned beef and sardines. He had never been so rich. When the coffee boiled, Nebu took Gibson's cup and held it out. The boy took up the pot and poured steadily.

The boy had shrill music he was listening to. It was louder than the rough swish of water through the trees, secret and splendid. This music never ran up and down like the music the Others tuned in on their wireless sets, but only ran *in and out*. This music came from the summit. Planetary stuff. It gave him the most wonderful ideas. One time, on the in-trail, when his father had taken him piggy-back through the bush, he had heard the music. After that, his father used to tie his hands when he took him piggy-back.

"I like camping at night," he said, while the black waited wordlessly for him to fill the cup. "The children in Nairobi say I am like the gekko lizard. You know the gekko lizard? The ones with the gray skins who croak at night? The children in Nairobi say I am like that lizard and I used to croak for them and unskin my eyes. You want me to unskin my eyes? To croak for you?"

He held the pot away and worked his childish mouth into the hideous pucker of the gekko and gave the *urk urk urker urk*, his eyes bright on Nebu.

"And would you like to hear mc laugh like the hyena? Or bark like the bull alligator?"

Nebu stared into the fire, hurt and bewildered. The payment he was making was not enough. For although the law said only that it should be flesh, the law also meant that it should be flesh you would be sad at, or made poorer by, losing. Like your fat cattle or she goat, or in the supreme coin, a wife of great comfort. Not even was the punishment enough for what he had done to the bwana; for the hole in his side contained only a beetle. In some wounds a lion roared, or a leopard clawed itself; and in the death wounds whole herds of elephants uprooted within. The half bwana was a thin coin. Making recompense through such a boy would be cheating his way out of a debt. A son from the Masai girl would have been ample payment. She had limbs that made her sweet-moving as a slow river, a proud river. She broke like a queen and at that time you knew that a son of her would be coin from the mint, firm, unhandled.

Nebu sucked in a great gulp of the washed air drifting into the cave. He looked at the cocky gray animal who was slyly regarding him from the other side of the fire. Nebu knew the boy had been mocking him. He ducked a toe at the pack on the ground.

"Do you read the bwanas' God-book?" he asked softly.

The brown doors flashed open. "You mean the Bible?"

Nebu remembered the old chief in the Adult Class. Redoubtable at debate in the tribal councils, the old man had plodded through the English books until he was as invincible on the bwanas' own ground. He used the words he had heard the old chief use to a European policeman.

"Where-fore," Nebu said awkwardly, "let him that think-eth he stand-eth take heed lest he fall. First Co-rin-thi-an ten twelve."

The boy clapped his hands and it echoed far back in the cave. "Bravo!" he cried, hearing the music very shrill and loud.

Nebu grunted and ran his finger lightly around the ruffle of the wound's mouth, inside which the beetle was kicking up an itch.

Chapter 13

T HE RAIN SMASHED on the stoop of the cave and exploded into spray. Moths died valiantly in it, struggling toward the fire brightly burning in the cave. Nebu, a blue-black god squatting quiet beyond comprehension, watched the pink-wings and the house-builders and the long-horns and red admirals and all the little ones hurrying so devotedly into the fire. One alighted on the barrel of the rifle and folded its wings. It was fat, and pollen lifted from it into the air currents. *A weakling*, leaped the thought into Nebu's head. *Without spirit. Afraid to die.* He watched the unflinching ones enter the flame.

He took up the rifle and shook off the fearful one. The boy's head snatched out of the air and whipped around to watch him. Nebu put the barrel to his cheek and jerked the rifle on the moth's erratic course. The moth settled on the boy's forehead and Nebu snapped the rifle into position and pulled the trigger. *Bang*, he said gravely. Angrily the boy slapped his forehead and squashed the moth.

"I killed him," Nebu said. "The weakling is dead."

The boy looked into the mouth of the gun and the gray face whitened and the nostrils were pinched.

"You are in a mess," he said thinly at Nebu. "You are one Kikuyu in a mess. The white soldiers will kill you presently."

"The insect is dead," Nebu repeated. "You saw me kill him?"

Those brown doors slipped open in the boy's eyes and the black leaned forward carefully looking for signs.

"You will never kill even a wish with that rifle!" he cried, shrill with it. "My father was better than you, any day! Any time! He filled his pot and brought in any number of trophies too! See—he was a white man! You understand, nigger? He was a white man. That rifle is spooked for you, Kike!"

Nebu had it well stoked down. Soft was his voice stroking toward the boy. "The worms know no color. And they stay underground when the long rains descend. But they will be occupied. Tomorrow the bwana will be without skin. The Great Father will not know him from me." He had spoken in Kikuyu and now he was musing, hunched down with old truths like a prophet.

"That is the way of the Great One. We stand before him without skins. None is black, or white either. It is a mystery."

"You are carrion!" the boy cried in that tongue.

And Nebu jerked under it, from head to toe. Then he recovered and looked away for a time as long as it would take to count up to twenty. But once again he looked at the boy. "You speak my tongue," he said in Kikuyu, solemn as bread. "I am made happy to know that you speak my tongue."

The boy made the same little formal bow which Nebu had given him and it was as if they were at a tea. But he was all raw wires and sufferings inside. Nebu opened the jacket and scratched around with a finger and the boy saw there was a mouth to the wound.

"I would open that wound if I were you," he said compassionately to the black, "and let out some of that pus."

He had the Negro staring blankly at him. "The—pus?"

The boy took himself into hand and drew a seraphim's face out of his gray, drawn looks. "The bad water," he said graciously. "The pus. The water that kills."

"It is a weak wound," Nebu replied after a while. "A beetle." His finger went with husbanded energy around the itching wound.

The boy chortled amusedly in his belly. He was a one. Why did he think the black would allow him to open the wound? Why did he think the black trusted him? When he grew older he would use a knife. It must be a noble feeling to use a knife slowly and skillfully, watching the victim's face all the time. He had done it once on the setter bitch owned by the Red Bull of a man who had been his father, but his father had nearly killed him for it. And anyway, the face cut from lumber had never showed a thing. Only opened its mouth and yelped something bitchy. The black's face would have shown it. All that goddamn smooth skin would have crackled like stiff tissue gripped in your fist.

"You go to the white man's school?" Nebu asked suddenly.

The boy grinned. Really, would he quote Scripture again? "I go to the white man's school," he agreed.

"And to his church?"

"*And* to his church."

"And eat at table with them?"

Face full of childish malice. "And eat with them, General Nebu. Do you?"

"And play with his totos?" the black asked eagerly. "His children?"

The high music was singing in the boy. Singing tall as a needle in his brain. He listened keenly to it and marched his fine, strong legs unstumblingly after the tuneful guidons, in and out among the booming, echoing stars. He was at home in the high, rushing light-roads and he knew them as he knew his numerals. *Eleven plus thirty-one equals forty-two multiplied by thirteen equals five-forty-six divided by seventeen equals thirty-two point one-one-eight to the nearest decimal.* He was at the foot of the Second but he could do the maths the boys did in the Fourth Standard in his school. What did this addled nigger think? He hugged his thin chest in his arms.

"It is *I* who will not play with *them*, you black fool!" he shrieked at Nebu.

Nebu poked more wood into the fire and took the edge off the chill in the cave. The boy spoke Kikuyu and yet was one with the bwanas. It helped that he was proud, too. When you stole from a man's house, the good recompense was to return the value of the goods you had stolen, or better. The bad requital was to return something less in value. The sick little half bwana had acquired more value by speaking the Kikuyu tongue. He would take more of Nebu with him when he returned into the white man's camp. Perhaps as they journeyed through the bush something more of value would turn up. Nebu spoke affectionately to the Great One about the fleck of sunlight which had fallen on him, and took up the rifle again. But the Great One smote his knuckles and his fingers slipped from the rifle. He nodded. He clearly understood.

He should not be pushing. It would be ascertained in his head when the Great One was satisfied.

He drew the rifle beside him and rolled himself in the blanket and lay down, feet toward the fire. The beetle was active in his side. This pain, too, was recompense. It was the law.

Chapter 14

IN THE NIGHT, the wood was eaten wider and the fire shrank, and the boy lay awake listening to the rain. The shadows in the cave overpowered the light and squeezed it to a slit around the embers. Outside, the savagely hungry floods tore away and swallowed chunks of earth big enough for an earth-quake to eat. Great boulders crashed like siege guns.

It was like telling lies in the confessional. That was it. Bad as telling lies in the confessional not to have made something happen to the silly black long ago. One could have understood his failure where his father was concerned. Tying his hands every night was no joke. But he had turned it neatly. Going to his knee each night in the boma, the fingers interlaced above corded hands, and his face made into a seraphim just like those on the walls of the church in Nairobi. And then putting down the mas-sive cornerstone of the "Our Father" and strewing

the ten graceful "Hail Marys" round and round it . . .
"*Blessed* art thou amongst women and *blessed* is
the fruit of thy womb, Jesus . . ." and how the Red
Bull used to squirm! *"Pray for us sinners, now,"*
looking full-eyed into his father's face. But the Red
Bull had not been ninnied, ever. The hands had remained tied together. And now, here he was, free.

He turned his head to shoot a glance at the black.
Slumber had collected Nebu into the blanket, tight
as a sausage.

Nebu slept like his land, the unlooted portion of
the forests and rivers. His eyes were closed and only
the gentle heaving of the blanket showed that life
was thereabout. His sleep was in rhythm with the
land, and if the rain had ceased or the wind had died
he would have instantly waked. As he did just now
when the continent tilted toward the sun.

He slipped out of sleep as he had slipped into it, a
brush of a feather, but an aura from the boy collided
with it and the warning made the gray face work
insanely as the boy sank back into his bed. The
black's eyes quickly roved the cave and went to the
door where the dark flood descended. There was no
light there but Nebu had *heard* the dawn coming. A
lizard, wet and shivering under a leaf, had croaked
of it. A big cat, nervous of the water, had coughed
it. He sat up and put wood into the fire and the
shadows leaped away.

The beetle had grown a beard in the night. It
was older, had grown a beard and was clawing its
boots for balance among his entrails. Pain foamed
in his bowels. When the Masai men in the bush grew
past forty, the hard young tribesmen walked away
from them and they were left to their old women

and the lions. Then they built a boma near a stream and blocked dung into bricks and built a hut and waited in the boma to die. You came upon them sometimes, hawk-eyes dusty, veined, their bones proud at knees and elbows, their bellies like footballs gurgling with wind. And they held their spears not like sunbeams straying through their fingers but like butchers' hatchets in the meat market. They tethered their cattle and threw away their bullwhips.

As I remember the great illumination of the moon at the ngoma when I was made a moran, a young warrior, so I remember my first going with Koko and what the bullwhips did. We caught the white special constable on the road outside the market and knocked him on the head and took him into the bush. That was the time of the Strange Feeling.

"Look at him, all of you!" cried Koko at us, the new ones, touching the bright yellow khaki of the young settler with his stick. "Look at him and undergo the Strange Feeling."

And the white constable had folded himself into a bright yellow ball in the mud and looked up at us in terror.

"Bow down to us, to Africa—you unlikeliness!" screamed Koko at him. "Free my young men of the Strange Feeling—teach them how to stand while the bwanas kneel in the mud!"

And he signaled by a snap of his fingers to the young men with the bullwhips, who slowly tore the flesh from the policeman. They tore his clothes first, the buffalo-hide whips cutting through cake. Mar-

*velously they undressed him, a baby in a tub, while
he squirmed and wept and shrieked in the filth.
And the morani, who had been magnificent cattle
boys before the Emergency, spilt not a drop of
blood until he was divested, and even then the blood
came in pin pricks, in precious rubies.*

The Negro stretched his cramped legs nearer the
fire and the wound clamored at his side. He drew
down the blanket and lifted the end of the jacket
and saw the gay flush of poison in his flesh. It had
swollen to fist size in the night. He warmed his
hands at the fire and pressed them around the mouth
of the wound. The agony made his teeth slip sideways. He stepped out of the blanket and went to the
door of the cave. He gathered wet clay and made a
fresh poultice. The pain spurted under his fingers.
He looked up and the day looked back at him from
slitted eyes at the top of the trees. He returned to the
fire.

The boy sat up and said, "Just listen to that
rain."

Nebu stirred the soup he had poured into the pot
from a paper packet.

"My father said that in England, on a day like
this, someone would come along and say, 'It's a fine
day.' "

Nebu put down the spoon and looked at the boy.
He said in Kikuyu, "Fine days happen in the heart,
toto."

The boy laughed and switched to Kikuyu. "You
must have been a priest in your village before you
turned bandit."

"All priests are bandits and all bandits are priests. All chiefs are beggars and all beggars are chiefs. Men are what they are when they are."

The boy's eyes shone. He spoke merrily. "It's smashing to know you feel like talking. Is it because we are speaking Kike? Or are you like this only on rainy days? My father said the niggers went crazy on the nights of full moon, or at the commencement of the long rains. Is it true, General Nebu? Do *you* run amok in the long rains?"

It went past Nebu and disappeared through the mouth of the cave. A bubble rose in his head and he pricked it with the thought that the toto may have eaten a pie of parrot. The toto could not know what had happened.

"Golly, I would like to see you run amok," the boy said, an engaging grin on the thin gray face. He rocked back on his buttocks and gripped the crippled foot like a satchel under his arm.

Nebu finished the broth and took it from the fire and poured it into two bowls. He handed one to the boy. "Eat, toto of the long tongue. We go far today."

The grin slipped mockingly down the boy's face. It raised itself when he put the bowl to his mouth and it looked at Nebu over the edge. But Nebu ate and walked his mind over the trail ahead today. The rivers would be fat and murderous now that they were strengthened by the rain. He would go the long way, circling the rougher rivers. He was growing a garden at his side. He could feel the flowers growing, gay poison flowers. He felt the mocking slice of the boy's eyes carve criss-cross over his face. He gave no sign that he felt it.

"What do you expect to gain from me?" the boy asked suddenly. He was holding the bowl waist high, gazing at Nebu. "Ransom? Like in the books?"

The word for ransom is the same for loot in Kikuyu and the laughter at it left Nebu's head, stepped a yard out and looked at him, and jumped back in again.

"I have nobody, you know. Nobody at all," the boy said sadly. "You killed the only one I had."

"Eat," the black said harshly.

The boy's fingers opened and the bowl fell, spattering and causing some hissing disturbances at the edge of the fire. Seated on the horn of the moon, he looked down at Nebu. "Your voice was like my father's," he said up there.

Nebu picked up the fallen bowl and put it, telescope fashion, into his own. He handed them to the boy. He took the ends of the four-in-hand straps on the pack and spread them on the floor and threw in the foreign treasures: the pairs of socks cruelly balled, the clean but limply folded shirts and undergarments, the crafty razor hiding in its case.

"The bwana could have killed me instead," Nebu said to himself as he worked. "So what is death? Death is to be slow for life. It is to have been slow in escaping the arrow or the sleeping sickness or the falling tree. Yet a man cannot fail to be slow, at some time. It is the law."

He worked at the thought solemnly, wonderingly, as at a poem. "Sometimes the wind flees ahead of the rain and then it slows for a mountain and is touched by the swordsmen. But does the wind die? The wind is not dead. It has gone into the rain. O, now, the rain is cavalry of the royal household, pennants flying, silver hoofs hitting, and the old bent earth slips backward, backward, curved at the spine, cowering."

He said, slapping the soft leather of the bwana's mosquito boots, "When Nebu dies, a part of him will enter Koko, or, maybe, someone else, to make him stronger. A man is never sure. Just as he is unsure to whom will ultimately go that portion of himself when he tires and dies on top of a woman."

He rubbed the soft leather. He felt it coming. "Life is like the wind, blowing equally, first from the east and then from the west. It withers, but never dies." And at last the *white* imagery strutted loudly forth: "Like the endless strings of sausages hung in the great stores of Nairobi, all their withered ends meeting to puff fatly again."

"God love a duck!" the boy whispered in English.

Nebu finished the straps. He spoke to the boy the formal words which opened a journey. "Let us look around the corner, toto."

Chapter 15

"IT IS THE wound," the boy said softly, swinging like a question mark on the crutch as he halted and looked carefully at Nebu's face when the black stopped. "It has the poison in it."

Since they had started, the wound had glowed dully at his side; but just now he had slipped and the wound had burst into light, shedding pain in him. He held it and sweated. Nebu listened to the agony talking in him and waited for it to be silent. He wrote it in his head that the toto had a false face.

The day dragged itself down through the trees, pale, sickly; the sun had no blood for it. The wind was axing the underbrush out of the rain but Nebu knew it would strike down again, for it was so the long rains fell. For a time, it would hector like a shrill wife and then grow tender, as it now was. But when you bared your head to it and held out your hands for it to anoint, suddenly it drove down again, brutally, tearing your faith into shreds. Life sometimes fooled you as adroitly as the rain. Like the lakes down on the plains whose placid lovely surfaces were roofs to bull alligators.

Now the pain was falling soft as pine needles and Nebu went on ahead of the boy. Far off, the rain sounded. They were crossing a neck of tall grass and in it was an island of bamboos, aloof as cats. He chopped down his hand for the boy to stand where he was and he crossed to the bamboo stand. He swung the panga at some tall shoots. He shredded the shoots of spiny branches as he returned and when they had got inside the tree line he stopped and split them straight down and cut them into foot-long lengths. He found lianas and plaited two pairs of mattings. He thonged a pair to his own feet and fixed one to the healthy foot of the boy and the other to the end of the crutch. The boy tried it and he was solid in the mud as a pillar.

"You are very clever for a black," the boy said in English and repeated it in Kikuyu using the word "Kikuyu" for "*black*."

The rain sounded again and caught up with them and the trees bent over their heads and acted as leaky umbrellas. But they had the groundsheets up and the water poured down them, coming in only at their ankles.

"Some Kikuyus are clever and some are stupid," Nebu said in his tongue. "Some white men are clever and some are stupid. Are you a clever white boy or a stupid one?"

The boy spoke under his breath. Nebu unslung the rifle and turned it about in his hand. All of it, as he had seen in Koko's, was there. The oiled barrel which shed water like a duck's back, the unspeakably lewd mouth, the sober trigger. And Nebu made game at himself that although his rifle was the twin of Koko's, this twin brother was a man of quiet deeds and shrank from all public outcry. If he pointed this brother at that gnarled old wild olive and waited long enough, it would kill whatever animal that was, occupying the lowest limb. Then, as he drew nearer to the olive and identified the dark brown, wet-carpety abandon on the limb, Nebu sucked in his breath. The rifle dropped at his feet as his hands threw into motion. The heavy iron spear fell into his hand, balanced between thumb and fingers. One leg bent and forward, Nebu waited for the leopard's spring, and beyond the strangeness of awaiting the charge of a cat in a rain-shrouded forest was the knowledge like an angering, disturbing blow that the leopard was *in front* of him, *waiting* for him.

The big head swung, the yellow-green unblinking eyes met his for an instant before the beast left the limb in a single bound that hid it in the undergrowth. And knowledge further sprouted in Nebu that he was being stalked.

Chapter 16

Nebu found a cave before dark and he stacked in sufficient wood to keep the fire in good spirits until daylight. He built a pyramid of stones at the entrance, sealing it against animals, and then he looked at the wound and smelled pus. Toward morning, the smell came to him again and the pain with it. He stayed with it, knowing it to be bad, but unable to think of anything more useful than wet clay. In the village, the old women would have chewed herbs to poultice the wound and he would have healed. Out here he was a man past forty and left for the lions. Or for the leopard somewhere outside in the half dark, eyeing the fire and considering all sorts of brave thoughts except that of crossing the fire line. No leopard would cross the fire line. He would wait until you grew big with carelessness and passed beneath his limb and then leap for your back and sink his teeth into the place where your neck and shoulder joined. Stuck like a brown burr on a

cabbage. He remembered a leopard he had seen lop-
ing through the bush with a buck in its mouth. The
buck was still alive and the eyes were bland with
terror. And the leopard had watched the black from
the corner of its eyes, a warning growl bristling out
of the sides of its mouth. Like a wreath-of-thorn
design around the bone-stiff buck.

Nebu, wrapped in the blanket and lying by the
fire, remembered the whole globe of subjects, but he
could not forget the smell of pus.

The boy lay awake thinking of the time when he
had caught the mouse and locked it in the room with
the house cat while he watched through a window,
and the way the mouse had gone up, rearing, a tank
on hindlegs, but unable to obstruct the god-cat when
it smote in. The back broke, and the boy shivered
deliciously remembering the deflated buttocks and
the limp tail when it dragged its ruins in circles before it was speared for the meal. He remembered
when the cat was finished how he had gone into the
room and picked it up and turned up the paw and
stared in fascination at the killer thing now sheathed
and innocent. And he rose to his elbow when the
black turned uneasily and he called softly across the
cave, "Good morning, Nebu. It is another lovely
day, isn't it?"

Feeling very good. Uplifted. In a state of grace.

PART TWO

Chapter 17

THE LEOPARD CAME out in the afternoon. It came out of a clump of husky chestnuts, off a low limb, and it was cold and wet and murderous. Save for the quick scrabble of the claws on the slippery wood, it left the limb without a sound; and when Nebu saw it the hindlegs were already hooking inward for sinking into the boy's shoulders. It was an alien flicker in the corner of Nebu's eyes but his jungle senses instantly smote into action. He was quicker than the cat, with the upward lunge of the spear. But the flying brute curved magnificently in the air, striking at the iron as it passed. Nebu felt the earthquake in his shoulder, in his arm, as the point raked savagely, helplessly, along the turning, cheating, hard-skinned coat.

It dropped squarely and the forelegs hit and

bounded off the turf like rubber pads. Snarling, it pivoted on the hindlegs. The great head slashed around and Nebu looked full into the face of the cat. Hate, fury, purpose flourished like green things in the tawny face. Desiring Nebu. Rippling to tear him down. The claws drew red wounds into the earth. The claws were dirty, Nebu noticed. The boy whimpered where he had fallen to the ground and the sound drew the reptilian head around to him and the pouched lips lifted off the teeth.

"No!" Nebu cried.

Anything to turn the pouring eyes back to himself.

He gestured with the seven-foot spear.

"No! Child of filth! To me! Me! Carrion! Work for your meal!"

Like the nobler ones of the forest. And Nebu heard the animal purr and he saw how the end of the tail moved lightly and his bowels contracted as under a sharp blow and he lurched forward, yelling.

He would have plunged the spear into it but the leopard groped in the ground and found footing, hurled itself backward, and was gone with two bounds into the bush. Nebu waited until the crash of its going was lost to the clearing.

He turned his head up to the rain. The insolent rain splashed on his forehead and ran down into his mouth. He blinked it out of his eyes. He looked down, clear-eyed, at the boy and he broke at the middle. The boy was very still, very wide-eyed now, staring to where the leopard had vanished. The pain leaped into the African's side and he felt it go down into his legs, moving liquidly. Filling him with a great warm hurt. Majesty, agonized.

"It is you who smell of death," he said, tall again above the boy.

The gray face tilted a worried look up at him. "Why do you say that? Why?"

Urgent.

"The leopard spoke, young bwana," Nebu told him. "He said he had come for you."

The gray face became like the ash of a long-dead fire. A fire feet had trampled. For a moment the boy's hand fingered at his pocket. Then the brown curtains closed in the eyes, and hate poisoned the boy's tongue.

"Don't be a fool!" cried the boy, scrambling upright and gathering the crutches. "You are nothing more than a superstitious black!"

One of the mattings had dropped from the crutches and Nebu went down and re-fastened it. There was majesty in this also.

"Why didn't you kill him? Is he one of your native gods too?"

Jeering.

As the half bwana had said, he should have killed the leopard. He should have thrown the spear, the cat had been less than a buck's jump away. But the body with which he was so intimate had spoken in the clearest tones of the weakness in it. One did not hurl a death throw with the heart alone. One collected the blood and sinews and skill into a single sublime moment and threw with finality. He had felt the fault in his body when he had drawn back his arm, the fault that had been placed there by Bwana

Gibson's bullet. He might have wounded the beast. But a whelping she-lion was a newborn lamb, compared with a wounded leopard.

"I should have used the white man's gun to protect his toto," Nebu said. "Then the white man's god would have relented and made the gun speak for the white man's son."

The boy's eyes drove daggers into the back of the black's bowed head, for he thought he had heard mockery in the Negro's voice. His hip was smarting, where he had hit the ground when fright threw him, but he had seen the leopard before Nebu had. He had even seen it just before it left the branch, for he had been a little behind and to one side of Nebu. But it had not occurred to him that the cat had been after *him*. And it had been, afterward, the oddest feeling, watching the stinking, muscular arms opening to embrace him, to see the claws coming out of their sheaths, slow as a girl's grin while she wondered whether to hurt you. The black had been quick, he could say that about him. But to be now *mocking* him! Unthinkable. The injury paraded kingly through him as he glared down on the curly head.

He said, when Nebu straightened, "The rifle is useless to you. Stick to your primitive weapons. Your bow and arrows. What about your bow and arrows? Why didn't you use this big bow?"

"One does not walk the forest with a loaded bow."

"The white man walks the forest with a loaded gun. The black walks the forest with an empty bow," the boy said understandingly.

"And so there are accidents," Nebu joked, still-

faced as a stone. "Has the young bwana ever heard
of a black man killed accidentally by a bow? Or a
spear? These are made for Africa."

"Yet the white man's guns kill your spearmen!"
the boy cried furiously.

"Numberlessly," Nebu said quietly.

He stalked forward, holding the pain in him and
thinking how it was like the hourglass inside the
Bwana Gibson's house. When it was drained out,
you turned it about and it was born again. The pain
should drain from his body and leave him clean of
sand as was the upper half of the glass. To make his
blood flow pure again, the muscles quick, eyes clear,
to make him cope with the bush and the strange toto
who walked with him. Tomorrow, he hoped to be up
at the sulphur pool, the place of big healing.

The rain lashed with more violence and the wind
bustled the larger trees and bent the saplings double.
He adjusted the rubber sheeting over his head and
watched the gray old face of the boy peer anxiously
out of his cape at the dark, whirling world. In the
yellow-shot dark of the rainstorm, Nebu saw the
erect pink flowers of chestnuts and the laburnums
beaten into the mud, and the leaves of the wild figs
thick and deformed under the water pouring from
them; and he wondered, as he had always wondered
when he was a child, where did the lions and the
buffaloes and rhinos cower in the storm? And where
did the eland and the gazelles gallop to, when the
floods opened over their heads? And did the eagles
and the heavenly flamingos kill their pride and weep
among the rocks when the long rains loosened?

Beyond the limits of the land where the tribe hunted, marked by those humpy hills rising and falling three days' journey to the east, the sun first thrust up the straight yellow shafts and you could see them swelling with growth, throbbing and widening as the golden ball hauled its weight up them, until, fat with fun, the great globe broke above the hills laughing wildly. And the night ran howling off the land.

They had lain with their heads outside the hut door watching the day come, and they were young and unspent as the day, the final shards of glory swinging in their bellies, bars of music tinkling yet.

"I will hunt and fish and work in our garden," he had said. *"And by the winter I will have earned the cattle and sheep for the dowry."*

"I will wait while my man does all these things," the new-made woman said, *"and bear his children when he returns."*

"They will be great men, these children," said the new-made husband.

"And faithful women," she said.

"And mothers of other great men."

"And other good women," she said into the growing dawn.

"Were you—were you—not afraid last night?" asked the brave young man.

He shucked his body into position to see her face. He wondered at it. He wondered at the strength there and was awed that he had heard her whimper. And he wondered at the composed mouth and unruffled forehead and tender eyes and he felt safe with her, as if with her he would stand boldly out among lions, or in the street of a hostile village, or before all the guns of raiding white men.

"The—pain?" needing to shake her, the old man-need. "The pain?"

"It had already been taken from me by the knives of the magpie old women," she said and they both laughed at the memories of the circumcision rites, and then were solemn at it too.

He said, "Tomorrow I will commence to build our hut."

"Tomorrow is today," said the girl whom the tribe had chosen to be his wife. "Today. Now, my lazy young husband."

But the sweetness was stirring in his limbs once more and today they would be undisturbed in the nuptial hut.

"Did you—hope—it would be Nebu?" the pride never really absent from love.

And she wrote the answer in her eyes and laughed deeply and gloriously and wonderfully hurt at his sweet ignorance. She had climbed lovely hills in the Nakuru district and swum the lake at Naivasha and walked through the forests bearing mountainous baskets of potatoes and bado and molded her body to be a princess fit for such a morning with Nebu. She would please him or disembowel herself. She would wash and cook for him, and carry his pots and spears, as long as she could love him carefully, competently, warmly, wantonly. But she would mystify him, storing her answers only in her eyes while her heart sang with the joy of it.

"A swallow flew in your eyes a while ago," he said.

"No," she said. "It stood and sang for you."

"For . . . me?"

"For us, and our sons and daughters," reading in the ignorant young man's eyes that it would be true, and she turned to lie out and look up at the strongly flushing sky through the trees, and the birds flying. And her sweet limbs arranged themselves to be perfect and good for him, giving much and taking much, in rhythm with him.

Chapter 18

"THE EVENING IS on us," Nebu said next day to the doggedly plodding boy whom he now made walk before him. "Tomorrow, or the day after, we should be on the white man's road."

"That is if the leopard doesn't get to you first. You smell of pus," the boy retorted viciously.

"Pus? The bad water? That is the smell of life, young bwana."

But he could smell it too, and the pain was rampaging. He had fought it all day, fought against a halt except for food. But his mind was now made up. He would pause at the place of sulphur. The clay had done the wound no good and he did not know the right herbs. Bathing in the place of sulphur would slay the elephants in his side. He had not seen the leopard all of today but he knew it was never far away. It would stalk upwind of them, prowling from branch to branch, taking to the ground when the trees thinned out but keeping to the tall grass. Pausing to scratch and yawn. Yellow eyes unwinking. Ugly head swinging side to side, alert for food or enemies.

"I—I suppose you will be taking me into some town or other," the boy said, cocking his ears for the reply.

"You will be safe when you are near to the white men," Nebu said.

"Not if you leave me on the road. There are wild beasts on the road."

"In the towns too," Nebu said sharply.

The boy chuckled, getting it. "Yes, the white men will tear you to bits for treating a young bwana as you have treated me. Fact is, you are nothing but a wild beast yourself. My father said all the blacks were wild beasts."

"Who saved you yesterday?" Nebu retorted steadily, thinking, *Clack clack* goes the half bwana's tongue, only to bruise.

"The ransom," the boy said, crooking his pale face in a grin up at Nebu. "The nice fat ransom you hope the white men will pay you for the young bwana."

The rain had let up but the small trees showered when the wind shook them. The wind slipped, when it could, furtively out of the underbrush, bringing to

Nebu the scents of his land, the slow sweet scents of the night-blooming jasmine and the *mutoma* and the musk odor of the soaked hollows which had been abandoned by the animals. But he ignored all these, thinking of the boy.

"I'll bet you are sorry you are a nigger."

You would win, Nebu thought clearly. *You would win your bet because I am weakening and tired and I want the white man's magic to heal the great wound. No other reason.*

"Day after tomorrow you will be there," he said steadily.

Chapter 19

FIGHTING IS A *tiring thing*, Nebu said to the Lawgiver early in the morning. *It blares like trumpets in the beginning and then it becomes a cracked cymbal. It has a stale taste when you cannot conquer.*

Nebu had heard it early in the morning. The big drum that was his heart, pounding hugely, and the rapid beats of the smaller drums at his wrists and forehead. They enveloped him, deafened him; and he had the rushes of hot piping pain more frequently now. He turned, and it turned with him. He sat up in the blankets and it rose with him, this close bedfellow. It was difficult to extend his legs for the poison had drained heavily into them. His shoulders spoke to him, not strongly, but distinctly enough, that they were usefully with him; but the legs worried him.

The legs wondered to themselves whether the miles of mountain and plateaus stretching in front of them could be successfully plundered for the lord to whom they owed allegiance.

From his waist down, he had swollen badly in the night. But he was nearing the place of sulphur. He knew the landmarks and he was sure to bathe tomorrow.

The black braced himself off the floor of the cave and stood by the fire. The strong, indomitable neck flowing unceasingly wide into the arrogant head, hooded with the effort to stand. He swallowed saliva which tasted brittle. The cave was floored with pain when he walked to the opening. He looked outside and returned to the fire. He considered, standing.

"But you may win—if you can die," Ncbu said to the Lawgiver. The Lawgiver nodded, remote.

The boy was fitful, troubled, angry at the unknown. He felt quite capable with the black, but the leopard was a page he had not turned. He had not told this to the superstitious black, but he had distinctly heard the leopard call his name when he had fallen to the ground and the brute had whirled and looked at him. He did not know how the leopard could have got his name. Nobody within miles knew it. He had not even told it to the black. Then how could the filthy cat have known it? He wished there was something he could *do* to the leopard but he had not been able to think of a thing all the night. He had merely floated aimlessly up there, listening to the music. He watched Nebu walk to the mouth of the cave. The stink of pus was all about the cave. He could safely write off *that* one. It was the leopard that bothered him now.

"I'll bet you have scared him off!" he cried suddenly.

Nebu looked up from the fire and met the hard brightness in the boy's eyes.

"Good morning," the Negro said. "It is a lovely morning."

The boy grinned and licked his lips. He could hear the roar of the early downpour. "You remembered, General Nebu? That is what my father used to say. That is, I mean *was*, a pretty howdy-do. You think he will be back today?"

"Who? Your father?"

The boy shot up angrily out of the blankets. "You damn black! You dare to joke with me! You know I meant the leopard which your clumsiness made escape us!"

Nebu said gravely, "Speak to the rifle for me and then we need not fear Bwana Leopard's return."

The boy sputtered lightning words. But soon he sat down on his anger and grinned mischievously and said, "The spear is the black man's weapon. And the bow. Don't you *want* to use your own weapons? Are you ashamed of being a nigger?"

The bow, the wanderobo, was six feet tall and he

had cut the first from the heart of the *m'pweki* wood when he had returned from the bush where the elders had sent all the young men to be made, out of fortitude and fending for themselves, into warriors, into proud young morani. He could remember the day he had put away the bow and gone to work for the bwanas. This one, the wanderobo he now carried, he had made years later.

He took it up while the water heated and took in the buffalo thong a little because it had been slackened by the damp. He fixed his fingers around the thong and tested the pull. He felt the pull at his waist and it shrieked all the way down his swollen legs and he released it to thwack harmlessly back. The sweat pushed out on his forehead. His wrist was long and flexible and very strong. He gazed numbly at them, extended before him, and thought of his legs. His legs had been long and thin and fitted into the flat belly with distinction. Now they were gross. Fat, weak trees, like the Congo bean, blown up by air and water. A yard would be a mile. They belonged to the High Court judge in Nairobi. They were strangers.

"Not so good, is it?" the boy asked softly. "You should have made me lance it. Bleed out the pus. I told you."

A little sorrow, Nebu told his Kikuyu heart, *a little sadness, a stir of joy. A little of everything. That is life.*

And the Lawgiver nodded. He smiled inside. The water boiled.

Nebu lifted the pot from the edge of the fire and rested it on the floor. He dipped the end of cloth in it and raised the jacket to get at the wound. He shrank at the sight. The boy rose and hopped quickly to his side.

"Here," the boy said, "let me hold it." He took the pot and held it close to the black.

Nebu pressed the hot cloth to the wound and the elephants in there uprooted trees. The great voices of pain whooped in Nebu, and in the midst of the clamor he exploded.

The Great One must have glued the agonized little pieces together; for he returned from absolute darkness into agonizing light. Groping forward out of the ruins, he felt the wetness on his feet and then he saw the overturned pot on the floor and the boy crouched in a corner of the cave staring at him.

"You moved suddenly!" the boy cried, seeing himself crucified in the black's eyes. "It—it— slipped out of my hand!"

But in his head he was writing down how like lumber, a piece of ebony, the face of Nebu had been. Suffering unmoved just like the dog long ago. And he was furious at Nebu for not exposing the pain. What thrill was there if it was not exposed? The blacks were just like beasts.

The Negro stumbled forward out of the destruction and acknowledged the boy's words with a grunt. He sniffed and shook his head coming out from under tons of fallen rock. Under his lowered brow, he watched the boy closely. He was sure he had caught a glimpse. He breathed in sadly at it. It was as well that the beetle had left the wound and that the elephants were trumpeting now. The recompense he was offering was not suitable. Not suitable at all.

"Yet the young bwana accused me of clumsiness," he said gently. But there was nothing to be seen. The brown doors had swung shut. "Let us eat, and go."

Because of the inroads they had made into the stack of tins, the pack had been considerably lightened. Now Nebu left in the cave the foods they would not be needing for their journey to the road. He also left the wanderobo, taking only the panga and spear. The panga was thonged to his body, was a part of him, for he slept with it there. The spear was no more obstruction than his arm. He could not pull the bow. He also took the rifle.

His speed was dictated by the boy's hobble, so at first he walked comfortably enough despite the swollen legs. But the boy's merry chuckle was not unexpected.

"I think it is funny, General Nebu. Really funny," the boy said. "Here we are, a pair of cripples. Two cripples. I'll bet the leopard will not be able to make up his mind which of us to take first."

Nebu said nothing, holding in his strength. He was guiding the boy by touching him on the right or left shoulder with the butt of the spear; touching him on the top of his head when he wanted a halt. He had his own solemn humor when he had the notion that the young half bwana walking before him was a calf being driven to the market place to be haggled over, bargained with, the hock and liver bringing so much. He moved carefully along, keyed to swift action, in eyes and arms at least. The smell of pus was too strong to escape the leopard. Lower down the slope the hyena would join the leopard. But he had no fear of the hyena; as for a different reason he had no fear of the nobler animals who shunned decay. Without bothering to be sorry for himself, he knew he was decaying. The leopard grew more ferocious when he stalked the wounded or the weak. He gripped down hard on the iron in his hand. The song in his back and shoulders was comfortably near to the perfect tune he had known before the bwana's bullet struck him.

"Let us say to him when he comes," the boy said gaily, "let us say, 'Mr. Leopard, before you choose, think who will be the bigger meal. Think and choose well, Mr. Leopard!' "

Nebu guided him to the right, out of the tree line, toward a patch of limestone gleaming in the dusky, rain-swept plateau.

"Half of you is rotting already while I am sound," laughed the boy merrily. "So, General Nebu, you will have to fight for *your* life."

Nebu tapped him on the head and the boy halted. The black said, "It is the place of sulphur."

He pointed the spear to the steaming little pool in the basin of the limestone. "I will bathe the great wound here while you stand and watch for the leopard."

The plateau was covered with low grass and Nebu had no fear that the leopard would try to slip up to them. Leopards struck from ambush, from the low trees, or from the tall grass through which they made their famous golden rushes, the tawny coat blurred in speed to the color of dirty gold. The Negro carefully peeled away the clothes from his swollen limbs and stepped into the pool. The bubbling water turned milky when his feet stirred the lime deposits. When he sat down the surface drew well above his hips, warmly, a mother of great love. It clothed and fed him and sheltered him. There was a wound throbbing, but it was pain happening in another house. He could see the fires burning across the street in the other house, and there were strangers watching around the sick one.

He had commenced the slow, hard gathering of the dowry the day after, gaining the cattle and the goats as payment for herding for his father during the cold winter nights; standing taut by his spear in the hot, short days, eyes caked and burning by reason of the unending watch for marauding cats. And one day toward the end of the year when the long rains ended and the plateau came alive with young grass shoots friskily gamboling with the wind, he had herded the flock the fortnight's journey over hills and through long valleys to the ridge above the village. He had halted before the ridge.

Puzzled, young Nebu sniffed the smoke and listened. It came weakly up, floating bodilessly, the dum da da dum, *beaten with the back of the hand, the death drum.*

And, uncertain whether the village had been raided by the ferocious Somali, or had been punished by some punitive party from the white man's town, the youthful Nebu had crawled forward to the ridge and looked down. His village was dead. Hyenas slunk in and out.

The discredited witch doctor, who had failed to stop the Kaffir Pox and who had moreover fallen himself a victim to it and was dying over his drum, told him. What was left of the village had moved on, leaving the dead and dying. She had died early. The

*witch doctor, fully clothed in the deadly lumps, beat
the drum slowly with the back of his hand.*

"*The leopard!*" the boy cried out. "*Nebu—the
leopard!*"

The body that the black burdensomely raised
from the pool was heavy as an elephant's. He was
an old woman, stepping from the pool. The warm
water poured down his thighs, and the air, turned
cold now, dug him with needles. The boy was swinging excitedly on a single crutch, flapping his hand
toward the trees.

"He came out from there! I—I saw him creeping
toward me and—and—I shouted and flung the
crutch at him! Then he turned and bolted back
among the trees!"

Nebu searched the trees with his eyes but saw no
signs. It was the custom when you sought healing in
the pool to soak from dawn to noon, but the black
remembered the sick, sour body he had with diffi-
culty lifted out of the water and he knew he had
slowed up too considerably to be in the pool if the
beast struck. He had better be on his feet and ready.
Awkwardly, he dressed, picked up his weapons, and
motioned to the boy to go on. The boy looked helplessly at him.

"The crutch—I threw it at him. It fell behind the
rock—there."

Behind the rock, where the clump of ferns flourished like a mass of green lace. He nodded, knowing
the hard going the soggy ground was for the boy. He
went over to retrieve it, stopped, and the mamba that
had been curled among the ferns struck. But the
frightened serpent had moved too early and Nebu

with a soft grunt flung it away before it could coil to strike again. Then, with a quick swing of the panga, he sliced away the head.

The smooth black mask face of the Negro with the eyes like unseeing jewels turned on the boy and went past him and Nebu looked out at the hills, which seemed engraved in stiffened smoke. The question stirred slowly in his breast.

"Pick it up," he said. A thousand years old he was. "Pick it up, *white* boy."

The boy's face was closed against the African. A queer dignity went with him as he moved forward on the stick, and he didn't seem to hobble at all. He picked up the staff he had tossed into the ferns when he had seen the mamba slither there to hide. He shook off the beheaded thing and wiped the wood in the grass. He tucked the crutch under his arm and swung around facing the Kikuyu.

"There was no leopard," Nebu said lonely, wearily, nobody in his house.

The clean-limbed athlete who was the murderer in the boy ran lightly out of him and swung to the horn of the moon. Grinning happily, he dangled his sound legs and listened to shrill music. Rain dimpled the surface of the pool and Nebu drew the groundsheet over his head and motioned the boy ahead. Protected under a fold of rock, a mile downwind the leopard rose and yawned and slipped out to the wet again.

Chapter 20

Nebu said to the long muscle that springs like a bow from kneecap to hip, "There are hills to cross today."

His head was filled with the hills, light green hills and dark ones, hills where buttercups blazed like yellow fires at dusk; hills that were long-drawn-out shrieks on whose slopes the best would buckle; and the wrinkled, mean, nut-brown ones that would twist your ankle and your soul. Yet Nebu knew that, save for the general upcurve of the valley he was in, upcurving to the *kopje* where the Nairobi road looped nearest toward him, there would be no ascensions to be made. Out of weakness he had spoken to the muscle.

And the muscle murmured wearily underneath the acres of swelling, and the black knew it would be cruel work there. Looking into the fire, he spoke questions to the femur and the fibula and the other bones he had known so well, that had been good to him in the past as the fine days were good to the hunter, as the old rocks had been good to the adolescent mountains, as the aged woods had been good to the proud new foliage when the earth came alive each springtime. And they too answered that they were frayed from the pain and the great weight of flesh they were bearing. Then, in a sweating panic as the mighty wound hit him with agony again, Nebu cried out to the Lawgiver in his breast, "Heart, do I take the half bwana to the white man's town? Do I have the strength to go all the way?"

There were fearsome moments to listen to the deliberations of the Lawgiver, to the slow lunges of the hammer in his breast.

"Is there a recompense to pay?" the Lawgiver finally asked.

"There is a recompense to pay."

"And who will pay the recompense, Nebu? Are *you* the Wronged One?"

"I am to pay," he said unsteadily. "I am to pay to the Wronged One."

"Then why do you ask? Would you abandon the rules of your fathers?"

And why not? shouted the weakness in him. *Can one-half of a man out-guile the white man's guns and fight the leopard and yet obey the rules?*

But the Lawgiver turned sadly away at his cowardice.

The pain darkened and Nebu keeled slowly over and thudded to the floor, six inches from the fire.

"God luvaduck!" cried the boy excitedly as the African struggled up and sat again, his back to the wall. "General Nebu—you nearly croaked then!"

The Negro said, an hour later, with his spear pointing up the distant swash to where instinct and a nose for the dwellings of the whites told him the road lay, "Just beyond that hill is the white man's road. If I fall you go on alone. You must go to the white man."

The thin gray face whipped up to him. "Alone?"

Nebu saw the terror crease along his forehead and down the sides of his face and run down into the thin bitter mouth.

"You black fool! Give me the rifle. Give it to me. I can use it. But you can't—never so long as you live."

He launched himself forward on his crutches. One birdlike hand clawed for the sling of the rifle on the black's shoulders. He tugged, screaming.

"You Kikuyu ape! You filthy, filthy ape!"

Tears flowed obscenely down his face; he fought at the sling, waking the pain in Nebu's side. The Negro stood immobile, until one crutch slipped and the boy sprawled in the mud.

"You will die, Nebu," he screamed. "The leopard will kill you because you stink. Then I shall use the rifle and walk alone."

He lay there shrieking, and hammering his face in the mud. Nebu stood alone in the land and held up his face to be washed by the friendly rain. He caught water on his tongue and drank it greedily.

He had been with several bands before Koko's and had left them as affairs drove him. One had been led by M'lodi, a thickset northern Kikuyu whom the British caught and hanged. The band had been pushed in retreat up the slopes to near the snowline, far from villages and game and women, as the British lines deepened in men and cannons and the planes wailed down from the skies and bombed them. And those were the Days of Ache.

"We ache in our guts and below our guts from hunger," M'lodi one evening said, brutally, as befits a leader. "There is little game, and no women. If we fire our guns it will bring the pink-cheeks on us. Be it known to all then: we will eat shrubs and be wives to ourselves."

And Nebu, although he had no cry for leadership beating in him, had wondered why M'lodi, who every hour cried that he was the leader, why did he not have the men cut bows and hunt game with them. He spoke to one of the spearmen, and the spearman, who feared M'lodi, told it to M'lodi to buy favor. So on this shivering cold day, M'lodi, in a terrible voice, called out Nebu before the band.

"Take off the white man's clothes!" bellowed M'lodi, jabbing the old pea jacket with his chief's stick.

Nebu looked around him, at the hard-set faces, and he knew the near thing it could be if he showed resistance. So he shed the jacket and was a defenseless fellow before M'lodi in the wind. And M'lodi danced with rage and shrieked, "Now you are a native!" and whipped him on the naked shoulder many times. "Do you like being a native?"—a word pulled out with his teeth. "Do you want to be a naked bush native again?"

Wealing his back. Washing his soul in pain and blood so he would be whiter than snow.

And later while he rubbed clay into the bloody weals, raw as fire, that M'lodi had given him, the

lesson was fixed in Nebu's mind that the Days of
Ache were also the Days of the Gun. He retrieved
the spear and took off from the camp. M'lodi had
whipped him because he had wanted to return to the
Days of Wood, the Days of the Bow. But as he went
down the slope and saw here and there through the
trees the gaunt male limbs writhing on each other,
a day's journey down, where the m'pweki trees
grew, he cut a sinew from one of the m'pwekis and
made himself a bow.

The unnatural M'lodi lost most of his troop and
the English caught him and slew him with a rope.

"The gun will not speak for you either," Nebu
looking down told the back of the boy's head. "The
gun is for the bwanas."

The boy flung himself around in the mud and the
brown eyes blazed up at Nebu. "Ignorant!" he
screamed. "Am I not a bwana?"

Nebu looked away, up the valley. He said
thoughtfully, "My strength will not hold. And the
leopard is impatient. Let us go now."

The rain fell quietly, austerely, silver threads
leaking from a fine-punctured leaden bowl. Nebu
thought of some journeys he had made before, the
golden journeys, through sunlight and shining grass
with coveys of francolins and spurfowl sporting on
the hillsides, and the orange-red redshanks wading
in the blue lakes. Some journeys had the severity of
silver, those in the months of the "small rains," the
cold December moon days. There were journeys
that were the dark journeys of midnight, with lighted
fires in your side and the flames wrapping your loins
and flowing down your thighs and legs and ankles—

and a stalking leopard unafraid of your fires. Journeys that ran dark murmurs through your veins.

Nebu looked about him and he saw that already the *teita* were out, blooming in fleecy white flowers that were born to scent the land only as long as the rains lasted. The rain flowers. And the *canarinas* were comforting the sad, sodden trees, climbing all up and around them and garlanding them with warm, orange-tinted bells.

And looking about he saw these too:

The scarlet, upflung heads of the fireballs' glowing defiance.

And the aromatic balsams, thick enough to hide buffaloes.

The many-fingered hands of forest ferns guarding the faces of the rocks; entombing those secrets hidden in the boles of dead trees.

And the blessed green hands of the *murichis* flinging cupfuls of fragrance and purple blooms all over the places he would walk.

Inside the earth, underneath his feet, inside the booming earth he felt the sliding and the settling of the humus fixing to shoot upward, to publish the tidings of a new creation. So in the soles of his feet Nebu prayed to his rude God.

"Almighty God," he said to his rude God, "make my limbs mighty to withstand the journey and the leopard."

He knew that stand of *mwena* over there. They flourished dark and tall and stout in their trunks and wore bright yellow spikes stuck fetchingly in their foliage. He knew the great gray baobab too. Under such a baobab had the tribe held market place and council place. And when they danced the ngoma all night until the sun rose, the whole company would shuffle and pound, moving sideways like an immense dark flower until they were beneath the baobab, in its shadow.

"Baobab," Nebu said to the baobab tree as the pain struck him and reeled him to lean against the bole, "baobab, the white man's bullet is making me beautiful. Can one who stinks so be made beautiful?"

The baobab asked sternly, "What did the Lawgiver say to you?"

Nebu would not answer. He turned to the wound and asked gravely, "Wound, O green garden growing in my side, is death to come when the flowers of poison open in me?" But the wound had its own rough ground to cover.

Nebu jabbed the point of his spear into the ground and came upright on it. He blinked, and saw the boy's eyes brightly intense on him. A motion of his hand signaled the boy on.

"Why don't you rest for a while?" the boy asked in a kind voice. "The pain will go if you rest. Lie down and sleep. I will watch."

The black grunted and motioned him on again. The boy stood his ground. Compassion was on his face.

"Moreover, Nebu," he said soothingly, "I do believe that the leopard has gone. For I tell you a strange thing: I cannot smell you any longer. It is healing, I am sure. Rest awhile and help it along, eh, General Nebu?"

But Nebu touched the false boy with the point of his spear and indicated with his head again. And the brown doors swung open in the boy's eyes and Nebu saw the swift leap of anger before they closed again. The boy shook his head sadly.

"Then let me take your panga," he pleaded. "All these weapons are too heavy for you. You mustn't fall before we reach the road."

The spear whirled in Nebu's hand and he slapped the boy with the flat of the butt.

"On, toto, on!" he commanded harshly.

The boy stumbled and recovered. He plodded forward, head and shoulders hunched against the rain. But he laughed silently and steadily as he went. *The black had been talking to a tree.* In the same unswerving way in which he listened when he swung on the horn of the moon, he was listening now for the African's fall. He had been *neat*, he knew. Contained. Implacable. The black would be *fixed*.

Nebu held out his hand for a butterfly to alight on it, clumsily flying with its weight of wet pollen. Half a mile downwind, the leopard smelled the tainted wound and began working upwind again.

Chapter 21

THE LAND ROVER, a sort of British jeep, carried a light machine gun, operated through a trap in the bullet-proof windshield. There was also a Bren-gun carrier, a World War II model but as effective against the Kikuyu type of firepower as a knife on cheese. The Army lieutenant had proof of it. He waved curtly to the men in the door of the police post and at the same time called out, "Let's roll."

The tiny convoy rolled out of the courtyard past the sentries at the gate and took the road.

The rain was pouring from a bottomless sky. The ropy rain tied the dark sky to the darker land, a liana-hung forest of water through which the vehicles seemed to hack a way. The Land Rover's blunt prow lifted and waggled and shoved ahead, the carrier lurching after it. The land no longer rejoiced in the rain. It took its beating sullenly, gloomily, turning uneasily when the wind blew. The lieutenant with his gloved hand wiped the inner surface of the windshield and thought of gentle Kentish rain and the smell of wet hops.

Chapter 22

NEBU MOVED HIS FEET carefully past each other, going slowly but with a proud bearing. He used the spear as a walking stick; with his head conical in the cloak, he was a seven-foot prophet journeying between cities. The boy swung on a jerky rhythm before him. Except for the occasional clash of a water-soaked branch falling through a tree, they were alone in a wet silent world. The black had long ago concluded that the big trunk muscles would be the working muscles. If a man could sit and find a wall for his back, he could fight off a leopard. He knew he was on stilts from the flexors of his hip joint downward: down there, there was neither anger, nor love, nor even weariness. It puzzled him that there was no Nebu down there, yet, when he looked down, there were the legs moving past each other, pompous as turkeys. He laughed at them, a huge joke bottled inside his head. But the big trunk muscles were different. *They* still held strength.

He wrote a poem to the big trunk muscles and sang it as he went pompously on.

"O mighty sinews, given me by my father and my mother,

"O massive towers that encompass the hills of my shoulders and the valley of my belly,

"O cry of power rising in me like the songs of a thousand warriors,

"Give me the flight of the hawk, to soar forever, because my strength will not permit me to be bound to earth.

"Give to me the roar of the lion, whose bravery will not consent for him to be quiet.

"Give to me the fortitude of the camel, to grunt only and not to weep when I am ill-used.

"Give to me the authority of the sun, so that none will look me in the eye."

He worked his shoulders under the rubber sheet and shrugged off the pools of water. He touched the boy, guiding him away from the trees. He knew that when the leopard struck again it would strike with even more ferocity than guile, so he kept away from the trees. It had been foiled before and the black knew that somewhere among those trees it was pacing them, now running downwind, now gliding swiftly in the other direction, tail twitching and eyes unwinking, pausing to wash its face and to yawn, standing so still sometimes it could have been a painted rock.

Nebu unslung the rifle and carried it at the trail.

Day before yesterday it had hampered him. He had noticed the imbalance at his back when he had fought off the leopard with his spear. Today was a weaker day. No day for a handicap. He carried the rifle along in his left hand and tried not to think how fitting the weapon felt in his hand. He looked down at it, brought it up nearer to his eyes, and it was all there, just as Koko's had been and not alien at all. *His* wrong must have been monstrous for him to have been afflicted with the great wound, a false boy, and a rifle that would not speak. He looked at it and shook it gently.

"No use praying to it," the boy's pert voice broke in on him. "It will *not* shoot for *you*."

He looks like the figures which the white men placed in their fields to scare away the crows, Nebu thought wearily. The shoulders that jumped up into little peaks each time the crutches hit the ground. The pitiably thin body as it swung between the uprights of his sad little house.

"Why will it not speak for me?" Nebu asked curtly. "Am I worse than the others?"

"Much worse. You will not trust the white man."

"Trust—trust *which* white man?" Nebu asked, flabbergasted.

"Me," the boy replied aggrievedly. "You have never trusted me since we met. Have you not been taught to trust the bwanas?"

The mask of head and face nodded in the white man's manner. "To obey him as he obeys his god who tells him to turn the other cheek. Not to repay evil for evil. Nebu has been wounded in his side by a piece of bread."

"You only got what you deserved. You should have stayed away from our camp."

"How could I obey if I stayed away?"

Sometimes it was better to joke than to write poetry. He could listen for the answers. Poetry fetched no answer. You wrote it in your head and sang it, just as trees grew and the blossoms fell. There was no answer to falling leaves. Except you called the new trees, that sprung where the leaves fell, the answers. And it was no answer; it was something new. Unless you thought of it as a cycle, without beginning or ending. The sap rose in spring, the trees flourished in summer, leaves fell in autumn, and the whole died when the snows flew. But again the sap rose in spring. Poetry could be like the falling leaves if there was a son to sing the verses you made, after you had died.

The African looked at the crooked question sign flailing along before him and he asked, "There are many magic things done by the white man's doctors; could they not have strengthened the young bwana's foot?"

The boy stopped abruptly. Then his back hunched and his head went down and he stood miserably in the rain. A thin line of wonder slipped into Nebu's head. He slung the rifle to his shoulder and reached out a hand to touch the boy. But he withdrew it quickly; and suddenly, uncannily, he was singing, a sliver of sound in his throat.

The boy turned the dead face up to him. "My father gave me a crooked foot, something special to mark me from the rabble. Do you object, *black*?" he asked fiercely.

The African felt the mud rising up past his face, drowning him. He looked numbly past the boy.

A sort of grin crinkled the gray face. "Don't you agree I look—different?" whispered the gray boy. "Where is your tongue? Flown away? Answer me, Kike! You ashamed of what my father gave me?" He looked at the boy. His eyes fell.

"The—the young bwana mocks me," Nebu said humbly. "He makes a joke at me."

The old-young face considered it. "Mock you? Joke at you? Yes, I suppose so. Only, stop asking me foolish questions and we will get along famously. You see, Kikuyu?"

"Yes, young bwana," Nebu said with his head down.

The boy regarded him closely. Suddenly he said, "Now I am a little weary. I think you should carry me. Bend down so I may climb to your shoulders."

It was two months' journey to the ground. An immeasurable space between his knees and the ground. A year of merciless days. A time of reluctant bones and flesh, and pain that giggled and shrieked in him. He murdered himself going to his knees. He floated up with the boy sitting on his shoulders. The crown of his head flew off and went whirling over the far hill.

"Go slowly, so it won't hurt much," the boy said kindly to the weaving Negro. "March gently, Nebu, so it won't kill you."

"Suffer," the black said to himself. *"Suffer so it won't hurt much."*

The boy giggled and suppressed it and said rapidly, "It is very nice up here, very nice indeed when you are high up. Look, Nebu! Do you know there are darters more than—twenty inches across the wings? When they are over the water, they fly fast and impale the fish on their beaks when they dive, then throw them up in the air and catch them again coming down. *Gulp*, they swallow him. Poor fish."

Few bwanas know that, Nebu cried proudly to himself. *Nor do they know of the sandpiper who is brown out of season, but turns mottled chestnut when they breed. Nor that the female of the spur-fowl also wears a spur. You can flush them by bark-like a dog.*

"I can see the fireballs, red as blood and marching with us!" the boy cried excitedly. "And the gloriosi are sucking the tall mutomas to death through their leaves!"

Few of the white men know so much. Few of them know that the monsonia *shuts in the after-noon,* Nebu sang triumphantly in reply. *Nor that the* mwethia, *the canary bush, grows ten feet tall and dies with the new moon. Proudly, I will bear you to the white man's road. You are a good recompense.*

The boy laughed high-pitched and happy. "Nebu! General Nebu, you are the general's horse! You hold your head high as the general's horse!"

High as the general's horse, Nebu cried happily, ignoring the terrible uprootings in his side caused by the boy's jabbing heels.

He strode gravely, stiffly along, walking the spear beside him. This was how he would have re-entered Koko's camp, head up and spear up, or no, the rifle princely borne.

"Procession!" the boy cried far above his head.

It is the warriors coming in for a big ngoma,
Nebu echoed.

"Procession!" the heels kicking into his sick body.
"Procession—the leopard has come out to join
us!"

And where are the lordly lions? the African asked
inside him. *And the fleet gazelles? The elephants?
We should see the lions going home from their kills,
bloodflecked and filled. And the old hippo, grunting
and rushing at his shadow. Tell me when the great
pythons curve from the bush, from among the sweet
scented balsam. Tell me what you see of my land,
toto. I would go blindly.*

The leopard bounded grandly from the balsam
over a hundred yards behind them and focused his
yellow-green eyes on the two humans ahead. Behind
the hard-boned forehead, there was just a faint
wonder at the fantasia of two sure kills who walked
before him and were not afraid. He padded on
calmly, only slightly put out that already one of
them smelled so highly of putrefaction.

"You carry me just as my father used to do," the
boy said softly to the damp curly hair, two fistfuls of
which he clutched. "You are good for a black."

Procession, Nebu cried to the agony inside, *to the
ngoma.*

Chapter 23

THE LEOPARD WAS a great dog at the mouth of the cave. Nebu and the boy were safe in there. The leopard loved them and would watch over them so that no danger entered the cave. Now and again the triangular head went down, sniffing unmistakably of the scents Nebu had left there when he had dragged himself across the threshold. The rain fell heavily on the sodden coat and twinkled in frozen drops on the nap of the jaws. It stretched its hindlegs one after the other, shaking off the water, and doubled the thick neck to lick the water from its underside. Nebu, his back to the concave wall, thought on the strangeness of a cat sitting in the rain.

He had fallen three times, or maybe four, but the boy had been very good about it, standing and waiting patiently until he had struggled again to his knees, before he climbed to his shoulders. He had been a good rider, applying the spur only when

Nebu stumbled. Most bwanas would not have been so considerate. He had long ago thrown away the crutches.

After Nebu had dragged himself to the end of the cave, he had sat down with the massively swollen legs stretched out before him, legs belonging in another country. They were beautiful things, greenish in places, large as trees, all the hollows rounded out so he had to guess where the ankles must have turned and the tendons used to make their quick labors. He bent at his waist and with his hands lifted one of the legs and wondered who the stranger was.

"The young bwana could borrow these for his journey to the road," he said.

The boy was wedged into an overhang of the wall. Outwardly stiff as ice, inside he literally churned with fury at the black for entering the cave. He had tried to keep him going toward the road but the ignorant Kikuyu had spied the cave and lumbered for it, unturnable as a mountain. He had tried kicking him viciously in the side; the black seemed to have lost the sense of feel after the first fall. He looked in disgust at the barrel-shaped body. The swollen nigger stank. He looked back at the painted cat and was instantly frozen with terror again. There was something he should do, but he could not rightly remember what that was. It was funny, the way the terror held him: he could *think*, but not move. He was *an effigy*, he thought brightly, fixed forever in gray stone.

The weapons were laid out beside Nebu—the spear, the panga, and the rifle. He breathed regularly and felt quite healthy. The cave went in deep, bulg-

ing at one side into a good-sized room. A couple of
large rocks that had evidently fallen from the roof a
long time ago, tall as a man, had rolled into the
bulge. He thought they would make an effective bar-
rier for the door but he was too comfortable to
move. Moreover, the leopard had come calling and
it was not tribal custom to spurn the visitor.

He called softly, "Brother Leopard, come in out
of the wet."

But he had spoken too early. Custom demanded
that there be a longer wait before you spoke. Brother
Leopard was a better African than he. Nebu lowered his head and looked hurtfully at the leopard.
A good cat too, lean-flanked and quiet. He'd bet
the coat was unmarred. That tail would be splendid
to flick with in the largest council meeting. It would
be worthy of a king. A token beast, well worth his
hide. The women would have clapped their hands
in the slow beats of applause when you portered
him into the village. The subchiefs would have
gathered about you and nodded the slow nods of
approval. And perhaps the chief himself would have
stridden out of his hut looking neither to the right
nor the left but long and keenly at the dead brute
and touched your shoulder with his fan of ostrich
feathers. But such things were gone.

The villages had gone, the chiefs were servants in
Nairobi factories and the women whored in Gov-
ernment Road. Left were just these: a leopard waiting at the door, and a boy cowering his false face
into his armpit, and poison warping your sick body.
He spat into the dust of the cave.

"Sing, blood!" Nebu sang defiantly. "Sing of the
strength seated in the back and the shoulders and

the arms. Sing to Brother Leopard to come, leaping in for his meal like the noble animals."

The boy shuddered and looked up out of the refuge of his armpit. "You said you would have taken me to the road. You have failed the young bwana," he accused.

"The white man's road is like the sands of Kilindini, unending," Nebu said garrulously. "Like the sea at Kilindini, immovable. You will go to the white man's road. You will cross it sometime, somewhere."

"When I am dead," the boy said woodenly.

"No," the African said, his face glistening in the half light of the cave. "No, the young bwana will never die. He will live forever like the white man's road."

"My father taught me your tongue," the boy said out of nothing and his body moved, unflexing arms and legs, shooting emotion into his face. "My father said I would never know when it would come in useful. He said most of the whites, being fools, never learned the Kikuyu tongue. *He* was a fool, but he was useful."

"Why do you say he was a fool?"

The boy rested the crippled foot across his forearm and leaned toward Nebu, his eyes shining. "You reminded me of him today, when you allowed me to ride you. All the way through the forest, after I had thrown away the crutches, he made me ride him."

"You—*threw* away the crutches?"

The gray face lost the light. He said sullenly, "Lost them. Why do you ask silly questions?"

A good laugh is like a free march, Nebu thought,

all your limbs joyous, hearing no sob in the cry of the curlew, brushing through the nettles grasping at your feet as if they were a field of daisies. The forced laughter in his head was like a forced march; the dust of it rose up to choke him.

"The young bwana lived in Nairobi?"

"Out in Parklands," the boy said, alive again. "A big house with many servants and I had a stout Somali woman to lift me up and down stairs. We got along famously. She never reported me to my father but she often cried. Her face was not cut from lumber, as was the dog's—and yours."

"The dog's? Lumber? Mine?" Nebu asked confusedly.

The boy was furious. "Who said that?" he shouted. "You are an ignorant black!"

The leopard stirred at the shout and the eyes burned steadily in on them. Nebu's hand silently sought the shaft of the spear. The boy froze in the overhang of the wall, his eyes blank with terror.

"Enter, Brother Leopard," Nebu said softly. "Let us begin our talk now."

The pain hit dully, growling deep and strong as an organ. The toto had lied. He was false all through.

Chapter 24

"TELL ME ABOUT your mother," Nebu said after a time of twisting and sweating and gasping. He was struggling up out of the bowels of the earth, calling to the first glimmer of light, identifying himself again with being alive.

But the boy's skin and bones were bondservants to the presence of the leopard. He sat still as the print in a book.

"I will tell you," went the voice in Nebu's head. "Her eyes were the sunflowers in April, blue as the *lipwe* flower. Her breasts were snow-covered peaks. I will tell you: on Mount Kenya is virgin snow and only the sunlight may lay weight on it. Her limbs were long and cool as the river. You hide behind the rushes and bathe in the pools, but it is forbidden to bathe in the open. She was a woman who lived beyond my ridge, a thought of last year's thunder, a whisper of a drum in the night, a bird that flew up from a far bush, a long-forgotten garden in which you planted your young trees."

He leaned forward, his great shoulders swaying, and the choir sang grandly in his head. "I will tell you. She was the forbidden road on which Nebu walked. It led to the hut of the king. But should a warrior be afraid of his king?"

Then his voice opened, booming inside the cave, rolling off the fluted roof. "A man should not love unless he seeks death. Love is death, Nebu. You die in the one you love. A little love is a little death, the big love is the big death. Nebu died the big death when he returned with the herd and heard the drum beaten with the back of the hand."

But his loins laughed.

"Loins?" he said angrily, and stopped.

He fell silent and looked at the animal in the doorway. It had not moved. It was growling in the uneasy halls of its belly. Cowering behind the growl was the mad scream leopards sometimes make. His long ebony fingers trembled on the spear.

"Which of them, then, did Nebu love big?" he shot at the boy. "She, or the msabu?"

But the gray boy was in a gray death, his limbs knotted and *still*.

"Loins," Nebu demanded, "speak then. Which did you love most? The girl or the msabu?"

"But I was blind!" his loins protested. "My eyes were closed when I sang."

"But was there any difference in your singing?" Nebu persisted. "Was your singing more splendid for the black woman or for the white woman?"

"Is today's rain different from yesterday?" retorted his loins. "Does it rain lead today and gold yesterday? Will the moon at next harvest be larger or smaller than the last?"

Ha ha ha, Nebu laughed, floating along on waves of agony, *I may not be here to tell you.*

"Then leave the question with your nearest kinsman."

The smell of what he had enriched the cave. If he had been home, it would have enriched his home ridge and the next and the one after that, all the land of the Kikuyus. The Council of Nine would have removed him to a far place in the bush and left him with his spear. But the Council of the Two, the Bwana and his Bullet, had done the same thing for him. A man is never, while he is on the earth, far from his home, thought Nebu. But there was no home in these lawless days.

There are three ridges in the land of the Kikuyu: Nyeri, Kiambu, and Muranga. Mine was the ridge of Nyeri, in the village of Kitusi, where the cook fires were never out. It was the law. We herded the goats in the day and learned to set traps for the coney and lesser kudu, for the smaller antelope and the bush pig. And in evening we sat at the feet of the elders and learned the steps for the ngoma and words of the old songs. This was the law. And we obeyed and grew and were taught the spear and bow and panga and not to lie. This was the law.

We did not stray from the law of our territory, nor from the rule of our chosen men in the Council of Nine. Where a man obeys the law, there is his home. The lawless man is homeless.

Ha ha ha. Loins, are you still alive? Have you got a home?

But his loins muttered vexedly.

"Bones," Nebu asked worriedly, "are you still alive?"

Some, the lower ones, were bound with dead muscles, but the others answered bravely.

"Trunk, are you powerful? Will you be mighty when I want you?"

He braced his shoulders so the blades met. His chest bulged like the corner-keep of a castle. The leopard twisted its head to one side and bawled into the cave.

Chapter 25

THEY HAD LEFT the vehicles a mile or two behind and had penetrated the valley on a short foot patrol. The lieutenant halted at the roar of the leopard.

He asked, "What was that?"

The guide, a crusty, fed-up-with-walking old Kenya hand, grunted. "Only a leopard. Probably made a kill."

The lieutenant, younger by a score of years, poorer by thousands of pounds, but God's vicar when on a patrol, said, "Let's go and hunt him down."

"What for?" demanded the guide angrily as the excellent coffee-planting rain ran off his helmet. "Are we hunting Kikes or leopards?"

"Good stalking practice for my men," said the lieutenant.

"But at this rate we will be out for a week!"

"It came from over there," the lieutenant said, moving forward. His patrol went in single file behind him. He grinned his hard grin and thought of the sad things: a lost dog, an odd shoe, a pot-bellied coffee-planter aching to return to his plantation.

The ground was soggy, but sharp-pointed stones stuck up like thorns out of the mud. He walked carefully, thinking God knew what He was doing when He placed pads on the feet of the cats. He wondered how the blacks managed to walk barefoot around here. They had no pads nor boots. God must have hated these blacks to have dumped them in places like these. He himself didn't mind them if they behaved themselves and kept out of his way. The thought made him feel magnanimous, kindlier than God. His big body under the loosely hung leather windbreaker drove ahead.

Chapter 26

THE LEOPARD MADE soft noises in its throat and its head sank a little between the forepaws. Behind, its legs scrabbled softly on the floor. The tremors ran from its stiffening tail along the spine to the neck. The neck was filling up, hooding.

"Toto, don't move," Nebu warned.

The warm rich blood was pumping forth along the African's veins, approving in a murmur the wakefulness of his biceps, saluting the great leaps of his pectorals when he breathed in. He felt the strength coil into his forearms and replace his fingers with steel springs. He was being acclaimed from all sides. Suddenly, the boy was unknotted. He looked at the black and looked at the leopard fixing its limbs in the door of the cave.

"He is coming in now," he said, far off as the South Pole. "He is coming in to eat us."

"He is coming in to die," Nebu said.

"You will miss. You are weak. I kicked you in the wound. You cannot throw."

"I can throw even when I am dead," Nebu boasted. "I can split him between his eyes, in mid-air."

He could split an elephant, with the potency he felt prowling through his body. He could tie the River Tana into a knot; or hoist Fort Hall past his eyebrow.

"I will split him so both halves will climb straight up my spear."

"You are a fool," the boy said, weary and sick down there in the cold. He held something out to Nebu. "Here—fix this to the rifle and it will shoot."

Nebu looked quickly down and then swung his eyes back to the cat. The toto was not only false, but a fool, too. It was a poor payment he was handing to Bwana Gibson's people. But there was no other coin. He had no goats nor sheep nor cattle nor beloved wife.

"It is the bolt of the rifle. I took it the first day. I have had it all the time," the boy said without artifice.

Nebu risked another quick look. But his head sang: *False! The toto is false as a worm's skull!* It was as the Bwana Gibson had said. He hated so deeply that he would rather see his true father die than live himself. The toto had been endeavoring to murder him back there on the trail even while he spoke the honeyed words. And even now, in the presence of the leopard which was making up its mind to kill, he was being false. Was there no limit to the boy's hate? Gently, not to disturb the fine balance in his body, Nebu shook his head.

"Nebu," the boy said softly. The black looked curiously at him.

"You love me very much," the boy said.

The boy's eyes were opened wide, stretched boldly wide so they were two huge, strangely lit rooms into which the black almost wandered. Nebu was glad that the great bow on his back snubbed on the threshold and halted him. His legs were sleek and firm once more and he backed away proudly on them. The Negro laughed in his belly; it was unseen on his face.

"*I* love you, toto?"

The boy said quickly, "I have thought it out. I know why you love me very much."

"The young bwana speaks in riddles," Nebu said gravely.

The ground was deep and springy underneath his feet, as it used to be. Through the soles of his feet he was sounding his continent and he could hear the wheat fields in the uplands rejoicing that Nebu the Farmer was back.

"Bwana, fiddlesticks," the boy grinned. "I know why. You are my father."

Nebu had grown out of the cave. He was three days' journey out of his sickness. The wanderobo twanged and the seven-foot spear sang, and game ran wailing through the bush that Nebu the Hunter was back.

"Father," the boy said softly, grinning at him.

Through the soles of his feet he could hear the ocean at Mombasa. The great waves stood straight up in the water, fifty yards out, and tossed their shaggy heads and roared in and shook the beach in their teeth.

The Negro said gently, "Then you know, toto. I would not have hurt the half bwana by telling him. For then you could not return to Parklands to the big house and play with the children of the white men."

The eyes of the boy closed tightly on the pain. "My mother was white," he said slowly.

"She—she was the woman of a warrior!" Nebu cried.

The boy's eyes opened. The pain was gone and they were clear.

"My father is a warrior," he said, his head up. "Nebu, the warrior. I love him very much."

Heart! whispered Nebu fearfully to the mighty leap within him. *Would you die at the good news?*

"A great warrior," Nebu said gravely. "Alone, Nebu slew a bwana who carried a rifle. It is a greater feat than to kill an elephant."

"You will kill the leopard too," the boy said quickly. "I know you will."

"Easily," Nebu said.

"Especially if you use the rifle. Take the bolt. I will show you how it is to be fitted."

"No, toto," Nebu said gently. "I know the spear. A great warrior is sensible. He does not ride a strange horse over a narrow footbridge."

The boy shuddered. His bitter mouth opened widely at the black.

"Fool! Filthy Kikuyu!" he shrieked. "I hid the bolt from you! Take it and shoot the leopard—now!"

Nebu bowed his head as the blow reached him.

He was back in the cave. He saw his obese thighs waxing in poison and smelled the pus. He raised his tortured face to the boy.

"No," Nebu whispered humbly. "Not again, half bwana!"

"Stupid—idiot—then shoot him!" shrieked the boy. The shiny bolt shot from the boy's hand to the racked, swollen lap of the black. The boy flung himself across Nebu's knees, fighting to get at the rifle, which lay on the far side of the Negro. Roused and angered, Nebu picked up the bolt and threw it from him.

"No!" he roared. "No—you are false! False!" he stormed. Then the cat must have given a warning to the African, for in a swift change of mood he said under his breath, *"Be still!"*

A sudden, almost unseen change had descended on the animal. Clearly, to Nebu, the leopard had made up his mind to charge.

But he will come in low, Nebu worried. *And it is much too dark in the cave to be throwing close to the ground. Come in high, Mr. Leopard, so I may have you high above the ground. Then there will be your large heart to split.*

"But no matter, Brother Leopard," Nebu said as he aimed the spear. "I think you will come as I want you. It is ordained."

And there he stuck, aiming like a fool, while the world doubled up in laughter at him. For with a cry curling back from him, the boy had hurled himself after the bolt as it twisted in the air. And the long, supple god made of leopard left the floor in a great leap.

"Toto!" Nebu cried from his belly, "flatten down, toto!"

For the leopard had come in high and he was good to get in the air. But the boy wanted the bolt—the little piece of luck he had saved to himself when, through struggle after struggle with himself, on the trail, fear had nearly defeated his resolution to be rid of the haunt which on that unforgettable day, at the commencement of the safari, Gibson had pinned on his back. With mad cunning, the planter had caught a glimpse of what lay behind the brown doors in the boy's eyes. He had allowed him no chances.

"Toto!" Explosively. Tearingly.

But as easily halt the tides at Kilindini, as halt the boy.

And the yellow eyes in the wicked head fastened larger and larger on the boy.

The cat bellow tearing from his throat, the leopard went up on his arc, forepaws up and hindlegs down, power and glory in the arrogant slant of the head, the exposed fangs, the three-inch claws unsheathing. And the final, shattering roar felled the roof on Nebu as the cat swept down on its mark.

The flying beast settled and Nebu's ear caught the quick *crunch*. The black lowered his head and peered at the boy and the slayer from under his brows. He was weeping. He blinked and muttered.

"Slow toto," Nebu muttered. "Poor, slow toto. You should have told me of the bolt long ago, then you would not now be in Brother Leopard's arms."

He broke into loud laughter and knew how strange it was that he should, at the same time, be weeping, and could stop doing neither. He leaned forward, shaking the spear.

"To me, Brother Leopard!" he cried at the reptilian head. "Here is better recompense—take me!"

The leopard growled. The boy was still. Outside the cave, the land creaked and groaned under the weight of the water. Nebu spoke to his muscles as he wept. He kept jabbing the spear at the beast.

Chapter 27

NEBU WAS LAUGHING his head off. The aloe tree in his throat shed bitter blooms of mirth up and down and across in him. The angry laughter rioted in his belly and in the rooms behind the bones of his forehead; and dug at the hinges of his jaws so badly he thought he screamed with pain. But the scream came out of him as a wild noise of hilarity. He could not understand it at all. He would surely explode, so hard did he try to hold it in. And he was cold;

freezingly cold. He wanted to be warm but he was already dead. The worms had got to him. The arm out there moving the spear so it tongued impudently at the leopard, holding him at bay, did not belong to him.

"Whose arm are you?" his eyes asked.

"The arm of Bwana Gibson," said the insolent arm.

The maddened cat raged at the cave's mouth. He looked unconcernedly at the cat. A cat being furious on a far ridge, unconnected with him. He felt roughened by the cold. Sleep would smooth him warmly out. But the choleric cat was entertaining, the way it fought and bit the air.

"Where are you from, Brother Leopard?" he called across the ridge. "Where do you rule, King Leopard? Did you cross the lands of the Kikuyus to dance before Bwana Arm?"

No. He shook his head emphatically as he laughed. No, no, no.

Not the lands of my people. The Chuka, the Mbere, the Mwimbi, the Embu, the Meru, the Kichugu, the Tharaka, the Ndia, the Muthamba, all the race of Kikuyu.

"We drew back into our forests, King Leopard, and dug our war pits and none could follow. We were invincible to black and white warriors. None would follow and we never came out. We were the Shy Children who stung when we were followed."

We burnt the papyrus to obtain our salt, and drank the blood of our cattle from the jugular. Our women fed on the milk of goats and bore children more numerous than the nuggets mined by the Great One in the evening sky.

His voice came stoutly out again. "You are strong as the oak tree," he said admiringly to the arm. It had a fine blue trunk and this wood would live for a thousand years. The leopard would be broken on it.

"We were the Shy Children of the forests, King Leopard, against whom the guns of the white warriors failed. But their gifts prevailed."

And he was suddenly clear-headed at that, and he thought, *A man's pride is mostly broken by gifts.* Peering at the leopard as it raged beyond the perimeter of the spear, he thought, *The pride of the leopard has been in his patience.* The cat quality of waiting. To go thoroughly away into silence and become alive only when it was time to kill. Patience was one kind of pride.

He said softly, "Your pride, your patience, was destroyed by the gift of the toto. You could not resist the gift of himself which he offered you. Yet your patience would have given both of us to you."

"Now you will eat neither of us!" he bellowed, lunging with the spear.

The cat hurled itself backward in a frightful uproar. It alighted and whirled fast, all around on itself like a top, furiously slashing its claws at nothing.

Nebu, ignoring it, looked down at the boy. He knew his land, its trees, and the savage life it spawned; and he knew that the leopard would not attack while he thought his victim strong and ready. So he looked down at the broken recompense on the floor, the twisted little cripple. A single down-stroke of a paw had done it. He had died quickly, quietly.

"What was *your* pride, half bwana?" Nebu queried softly. The bad laughter had left him. "To hinder as the crooked thorn bush hinders the foot of the traveler? Then you lost your pride, toto. You lost your pride and, instead of hindering, you tried at the last to help—even if you tried to help yourself. So, you lost, toto, you lost."

And it was as if he had written out an epitaph. He turned his head away, the mask face incurious.

It was fine that he was almost without pain now. Only the purpling shapelessness down there and the smell. He felt lazily good. Sleepy as in the late evening. As if evening, the long shadows, were lengthening in him. His head rested on Kinangop and his feet in the Ulu hills where the Kamba people dwelled. He laughed, sleepily, the length of his poisoned, dying world.

"But what is the bwana's pride?" he questioned sharply, his head on one side, listening. But nobody answered him. "Then I will ask in their cities. Property? That is all men's pride. Women? That pride also belongs to all men. To win? All men desire to win."

But only a few may win, went his head. Yet each one who loses helps another to win. So the man who loses may be prideful that he has won. The bwanas boasted of it. Even while they were being made beautiful by fire or the knife, they boasted of the others who would come after them.

"Then—then perhaps the bwanas' pride may be their strength in losing?"

It rapped smartly again for notice.

The strength to lose an age and gain a generation.

To lose customs, women, land, life, to the wring of change. And you could pocket a sunbeam easier than lure the march of change into a war pit. You could not defeat it. Each year, in the spring, change marched across his country, from Mombasa to the big mountains, and new flowers opened and new foals kicked wounds into the tender land. Change was invincible.

He said sadly, "M'lodi, the unnatural, had been right. I should have been strong and lost the bow, for the days of the bow had gone."

And when he felt the pain rolling back into him, he said to it, "Perhaps I lay here, hurt and alone, because I had not the strength to lose the old customs but must go to Nairobi to pay the recompense." The pain bounced inside his skull, and he gasped and said, "It is a braver deed, to accept change, than to enter the country of an enemy."

And then the jeweled eyes tipped right over in his dim face and he sagged a little.

"Nebu! Nebu!" he thought he heard the leopard scream, and the black jerked up his head. The beast was back on its haunches, tail straight out and quivering at the tip. The yellow eyes, half closed, had completed the calculations. Nebu looked lazily at the cat. Funny, what was happening in the cat did nothing to him: the shock ripples at its shoulders, the flattened, hungry haunches, the tiny quick movements of the hindlegs searching for the take-off. He only knew that the evening, the long brown shadow off the Aberdares, had entered into him and was disposing itself in much of him.

"Oho, Brother Leopard, evening is in my belly but bright morning is in my arm," he said softly.

And the formidable spear rose easily to his shoulder and power flowed along his arm.

I can throw, Nebu boasted, *from the Plains of Athi to the highlands. With evening sitting in my belly, even then I can throw.*

"Thank you, arm," he told it gravely, "I will dance at your ngoma, arm."

When his eyes open wide, he will come, sang the black.

When his tail stiffens and the ripples die along his back, he will come.

When the hood at his neck fills out as mine filled out when I sang my first male-song into the heat and velvet of my first woman in the love hut of Kikuyu, then he will come.

Instantly.

And he will die unquenched as my first love died.

Ready, Bwana Leopard, ready!

But the leopard did not come. For the Army lieutenant fired into the cave.

Chapter 28

THE ENGLISHMAN fired again into the body of the leopard and he was sure it was quite dead.

"Now let's have a look at what the bastard had cornered there."

He waved the men away from the entrance so he had some light as he went in. He saw the huddle of the boy and he stepped around the cat. He turned over the body.

"By God!" He was rattled. "It looks like a white boy... Shoes on!"

He stooped and turned the face up, his brutal hands strangely tender. It came easily around on the broken neck.

"Like a bloody muddy flower on a bloody broken stem," he brooded, helplessly savage. "Wonder whose kid was he?"

He looked around the cave. His eyes picked up the black at the end and he streaked to his feet, gun pointing. But there was no movement there.

"Robbed me of my first Kike too, eh, Brother Leopard?"

He raised the gun and considered firing into the black just to make sure, then he recalled that they both seemed to have been traveling together. This must have been one of the loyal bucks, perhaps saved the child from a massacre. He dropped his arm and walked forward. He stood out hard against the light from the door, a lean-waisted, wide-shouldered tawny bull leopard. And Nebu charted the curvature of his chest through the khaki bush jacket and marked where the breast-bone swelled above the heart and the certainty that he had the target well laid flowed sweetly through him.

Great One, the African sang in his head, *give us long knives.*

It was morning in his arms and shoulders.